A KILLING KARMA

A KILLING KARMA

Geraldine Evans

This first world edition published in Great Britain 2007 by
SEVERN HOUSE PUBLISHERS LTD of
9–15 High Street, Sutton, Surrey SM1 1DF.
This first world edition published in the USA 2008 by
SEVERN HOUSE PUBLISHERS INC of
595 Madison Avenue, New York, N.Y. 10022.

British Library Cataloguing in Publication Data

Evans, Geraldine
  A killing karma
  1. Police - Great Britain - Fiction 2. Murder -
  Investigation - Great Britain - Fiction 3. Hippies - Crime
  against - Great Britain - Fiction 4. Detective and mystery
  stories
  I. Title
  823.9'14[F]

  ISBN-13: 978-0-7278-6560-1   (cased)

All Severn House titles are printed on acid-free paper.

Typeset by Palimpsest Book Production Ltd.,
Grangemouth, Stirlingshire, Scotland.
Printed and bound in Great Britain by
MPG Books Ltd., Bodmin, Cornwall.

One

'*What* did you say?' Unable to take in what he was hearing, DCI Will Casey asked for it to be repeated, unsure that he'd believe his ears even then.

'*Two* suspicious deaths?' he queried. Two! They certainly didn't do things by halves. But then he knew that already. Such a proclivity had been the bane of his life for years.

He bit off a curse and said, 'And you say you haven't notified the local police?' He paused, hoping to gather both wits and patience, while he listened to the garbled explanation. But unusually for him, he succeeded in gathering neither, as his next words proved. 'Are you both stupid, Moon, or just criminally irresponsible?'

Pointless, really, asking such questions, Casey told himself with a grimace that he tried and failed to turn into an ironic smile. When were they ever anything else?

Illogically, he thought, *This can't be happening to me.* Only he knew it was . . . He really must have been very wicked in a previous life to bring such bad karma with him to this one.

He stared unseeingly at his living room. Gradually, his eyes came back into focus. It was as if his mind needed to ground him, to calm him. Without will or conscious effort, his gaze travelled round his living room till it rested on the wall to the left of the chimney breast and the place where his favourite piece of scripophily had once rested. The rare and – to Casey – precious old share certificate of the Stockton and Darlington railway had once hung, sacrificed to pay his parents' debts. The certificate Rachel had bought him in its place was interesting in its way, but it would never replace the original which had had a special place in his heart. His gaze moved around as he listened to further garbled explanations from Moon. This time it rested on the carved Hindu elephant-headed god, Ganesh. His mother had pressed this on him just before she and his father returned home the last time they were here. For good luck, she had said. He had tried to return it to her, thinking she and his father had more need of the god's protection. Even though she had laughed aside his offer and pointed to a similar, much smaller carving at her throat, he wished now he had insisted she keep the larger carving of Ganesh. Being so much bigger, it must surely provide greater protection in keeping with its size.

Too late, he breathed on a sigh as he told Moon he would get there as quickly as possible and put the phone down.

This time his parents had – by a country mile – managed to surpass any of their previous lunatic stunts. And, for the life of him, he didn't see how he could begin to save them from the consequences of their actions.

But, he told himself as he jerked his unwilling body into movement, grabbed his coat and car keys and headed out into the unseasonably chilly July night, there's no one else to do it, so you'd better get up to the Fens and see if you can rescue *something* from the mire.

The word *mire* caused him to pause in the doorway of his neat semidetached as he wondered whether he should change out of his new suit. But then, as he remembered his parents' two muck-attracting and neglected mongrels had both died within a month of one another earlier in the year, he decided such a precaution wasn't necessary.

As he climbed into the car, started it up and made for the Fens, he told himself it was fortunate he was on a week's leave. At least it gave him the time and freedom to try to sort the mess out.

God knew what he'd say to Rachel. He'd have to tell her, of course, he accepted that. Deception was no basis for a committed relationship and he and Rachel had been together now for some months. She spent much of the time at Casey's home, but kept her own flat on in the town. He was just grateful he didn't have to explain the situation to her while his mind was in turmoil and he was still trying to get his head around the grim events he had just been told about.

But as luck would have it, Rachel was out this evening. She had driven to Norwich with a woman friend to see a play that had been highly recommended. Casey hadn't wanted to go but had encouraged Rachel to do so, seeing as she was so keen. As a musician, between practising, performing and touring, she didn't get much opportunity to be on the receiving end of entertainment, and although he regretted the loss of her company, he didn't begrudge her the evening apart.

It wasn't that Rachel wouldn't sympathize if he told her what had happened – she had met his parents and would understand how they could have got into their current predicament almost as well as he did – it was just that he'd prefer to keep this business to himself until he'd extracted the full story. So he was relieved not to have been forced by her presence tonight to explain what the phone call was about.

Will Casey had always found the flatland Fens and their equally flat and empty approaches desolate, even during daylight hours. How had the Elizabethan writer Michael Drayton described them? Something about 'a land of foul, woosy marsh . . . with a vast queachy soil and hosts of wallowing waves'. Of course, much of the waterlogged land had been reclaimed since Drayton's day. But with the wide and moonless night sky louring darkly down at him through the mist that every so often lifted to reveal the flatlands stretching to the horizon on either side of the road as he drove with no light but catseyes in sight, he couldn't help but share something of Drayton's feelings about the place. He reflected that on such a night as this the legendary Black Shuck might roam the Fens. A giant black hound, to see Black Shuck was once believed to bring death within a week. With a shiver not solely attributable to the legendary hound, Casey wondered what scenes were waiting for him at his parents' home; a commune of so-called happy hippies enjoying their own version of Utopia.

Now, reality had entered their ramshackle paradise and it had suffered a mortal blow. Two mortal blows, in fact. And he was expected to sort it out and make it all better.

In the next rising of the murk, Casey glanced briefly towards the huge, star-studded Fenland sky and wondered whether he should pray to the Almighty or the Hindu god of hopeless causes . . .

Two

As Casey slowed his car for the approach to the commune's smallholding, he was surprised to see that the gate was shut. Not only shut, but locked with a large padlock and chain, as he discovered when he got out of the car. Casey presumed that with one body lying in a shallow grave in the smallholding's grounds and another presumably laid out in one of the outhouses they had decided to exercise a rare prudence. Shame it was a little late, he thought.

Amongst the usual collection of rusting old wrecks littering the yard, two of them still balanced on bricks as they had been on his last visit, Casey was astonished to see a brand new 4 x 4 that gleamed in the sudden light as the front door opened. Where had they got the money for that? he wondered. Unless they had a visitor. That must be it, he concluded as Moon crossed the yard to unlock the gate. Some wealthy patron who thought their lifestyle romantic. Deluded fool, he thought. But it was going to be awkward. Would he have to wait for hours for their visitor to leave before he could talk to them about the two deaths?

However, when, after his mother had enthusiastically embraced him and – a rarity from either parent – thanked him for coming to their aid, he asked Moon who amongst their assorted on-benefits acquaintances could afford such a car, she just mumbled something he couldn't hear and Casey didn't pursue it. He came to another conclusion: that their visitor was someone they would rather he knew as little about as possible.

Almost immediately, Casey heard dogs barking. Worried for a moment that the commune members had obtained more mangy, mud-attracting mutts, he quickly dismissed the thought; acquiring more dogs would require an energy and purposefulness singularly lacking in the commune members given that they rarely found energy for anything other than smoking dope and making babies. On the still air of this flat and otherwise silent countryside, he knew sound could travel some distance and concluded that the dogs must belong to one of the commune's neighbours.

Just as he had satisfied himself that he was safe from the attentions of uncared for dogs, two hairy and muck-coated specimens came racing around the side of the house yapping frenziedly. To no avail, Casey tried to shush them, only too conscious of the unorthodox reason for his visit, he could do without the dogs drawing attention to his arrival. With his attempts at quietening the animals clearly doomed to failure, he hurried after Moon, squelching through the mud, hoping that his disappearance through the front door would shut the dogs up.

As he trudged back with her, fending off the curious dogs and their sniffing noses, Casey took a look round the small-holding. And although the darkness was kind to it, the commune's property still looked as uncared for as the dogs. Daylight would doubtless have revealed the level of ramshackle squalor that Casey recalled from his previous visits: rusted corrugated roofs on all the outbuildings; the broken windows in most of them which had never been replaced; weeds which sprouted with vigorous, unchecked growth all over the yard and the land that had been left uncultivated as well as amongst most of the cultivated area also, which received only a sporadic and half-hearted weeding. Several doors still hung off the hinges they had hung from on his last visit. They swung and banged in the suddenly stiffening breeze with an irritating relentlessness that would drive most normal people mad. He could only suppose the drug use endemic among the community trans-formed the banging into the tinkle of heavenly bells. Or something.

The house was no better, he saw as, by the light of candles that flickered in the sudden draught, he and Moon entered the large living room and he pulled the door to behind them. The candles provided the room's only illumination and, but for the hall light that had gleamed out into the yard, Casey would have assumed that the electricity had been cut off again. Through the candlelit gloom, he saw two new settees and a huge plasma television which took pride of place in the corner. Even the carpet was new, he noticed, and replaced the one with the multiplicity of burn holes. They really were looking remarkably affluent for people with no visible means of support and Casey's gaze narrowed suspiciously as he realized that not only was there no rich visitor immediately apparent, but that his normally impecunious parents hadn't tapped him for a loan for some weeks. It wasn't like them. So what had changed?

Moon must have noticed his astonishment, because she told him, 'We came up on the lottery.'

'How much?' Casey asked before politeness stopped him.

'Enough,' Glen 'Foxy' Redfern replied for Moon from where he lounged full length on one of the new settees. His reply was abrupt and told Casey, clear as clear, that their lottery win was none of his business. But then he had always been a belligerent personality. Must go with his wild bush of red hair.

Their lottery win must have been more than enough, thought Casey, to judge from all the money they'd spent. And as there was no visitor in evidence, he surmised that the 4 x 4 in the yard was a new purchase of theirs as well. So why hadn't Moon and Star repaid him some of the money he'd lent them over the years? Disgruntled at this thought, Casey crossed the room, stepping over the bodies lounging on the large, grubby cushions that littered the new carpet.

One thing hadn't changed: like the outbuildings and grounds, everything was covered in a layer of dust, the original furniture a mismatched mix of colours and styles that no amount of brightly-coloured Indian throws could bring together.

Much like the inhabitants, he thought, as he looked around the circle of expectant, sheepish, drugged and out of it faces in their habitual well-holed jeans and shabby kaftans. He took the chair with the fewest stains and burn holes – the new settees having been appropriated by Star and Foxy Redfern, both sprawled out in such determined ownership that one would think they had never believed that property was theft.

While he gathered his thoughts, he examined the faces again; there were his mother and father, of course, Moon and Star Casey respectively, names which they had adopted long ago in their first hippie flush. They were by far the oldest of the commune members. Both were now pensioners, though one wouldn't have thought so from their irresponsible and 'opt out' lifestyle.

Sitting upright and tight-faced on one of the older settees was Dylan Harper, the bereaved thirty-something partner of the second victim, DaisyMay Smith; and across from him was Scott 'Mackenzie' Johnson, another, older thirty-something; and beside him, sitting close, was his nineteen-year-old gay lover, Randy Matthews. Then there was Kali Callender, in her early forties, the widow of Kris 'Krishna' Callender, the first supposed victim; and Glen 'Foxy' Redfern, next oldest to Moon and Star, with the wild frizz of bright red hair that had earned him his nickname; and Lilith, whom he called his wife, though as they had been married in a beachside ceremony of much spiritual significance, but probably spurious legality, Casey doubted their marital status. There were also still up, although the hour was late, several teenage children of the commune, whose names Casey had forgotten.

The missing faces – apart from the younger children who, amazingly, had tonight clearly been sent to bed at a reasonable hour – were those of the dead pair – Kris 'Krishna' Callender, Kali's husband, and DaisyMay Smith, Dylan Harper's girlfriend.

Casey cleared his throat and looked directly at Moon, his mother. 'You were somewhat incoherent on the phone, Mum, so let me, first of all, make sure I've got this clear. You say one of you found Kris dead in one of the greenhouses and have yet to report his death?'

Moon nodded. Unsurprisingly, her normal, calm aura wasn't much in evidence this evening. Even under the flickering candlelight that lit the room but dimly, he could see her fingers moving restlessly at her throat as she fiddled with the little charm of Ganesh, the Hindu elephant-headed god of good fortune. This time, his failure to work his claimed magic had taken on epic proportions.

Moon's eyes, too, seemed restless; the gaze from the still vivid green eyes that were so like his own, kept sliding away from Casey's. He prayed this reluctance to hold his gaze wasn't an indication that Moon was guilty of rather more than just the *concealment* of two sudden deaths.

Casey continued. 'And then, as if that wasn't enough to be going on with, for reasons that escape me, having failed to call for the police or an ambulance, you decided to move Callender's body to an outhouse before burying him in the garden. Have I got it right so far?'

His mother gave another reluctant nod.

But although Casey had claimed that the reasons for their actions had escaped him, he suspected that he understood the reasons only too well.

'Were there any marks of violence on Kris Callender's body?'

'None that I noticed, though I didn't look that closely,' Moon admitted. 'Besides, it was getting dark when I found his body.'

Casey felt a shiver of dread crawl down his spine. For that was the first time his mother had admitted that *she* had been the one to find Callender's corpse. Uneasily, he wondered what other unwelcome admissions would follow.

He already suspected that Kris's body had been found lying amongst the cannabis crop which he knew they grew behind the house concealed by a hedge, in one of the larger greenhouses, which location, for Casey, went some way to explaining their bizarre decision to bury him quietly without notifying anyone in authority of his death.

'Tell me,' he went on, although he doubted they would tell him the truth, 'how did you all get on with the dead man? Was he well liked?'

A jangle of voices broke out at this point, all seeking to reassure him that Kris 'Krishna' Callender had been variously 'a great guy', 'a hard worker, who always insisted on manning the market stall where we sell our produce, rather than following the rota as we used to', 'a gentle, benevolent, deeply spiritual man' and one who was 'in touch with the earth'.

Whatever else he might have been, Kris Callender was certainly the latter now, Casey thought. But, having met Callender a number of times whilst visiting the smallholding, he suspected the man's right to join the queue for sainthood.

'If he *was* murdered, it must have been an outsider that did it,' Foxy Redfern insisted.

'I don't think, at this stage, that we can rely on that theory,' Casey warned. 'Though I agree that someone could have come in from outside.' Their previously lax security made that a distinct possibility. It was the only aspect of this worrying situation that gave him hope. But even as he voiced the words he recalled the barking dogs: how likely was it that someone could approach the smallholding without the animals making a similar racket to the one that had heralded his arrival? Unless the mongrels had arrived after Callender's death. They were certainly new additions. He questioned them on this point; reluctantly, they admitted the dogs had arrived before Callender's death.

His mother's next words echoed his own thoughts and removed the last trace of hope that a stranger was responsible for the deaths.

'You're right, hon, the dogs would have barked. Especially Craggie, our latest arrival.'

Just then, as if he had heard his name and knew he was being talked about, the latest addition to the menagerie pushed the door open and entered the room.

Moon smiled, revealing stained, yellow teeth that with the long, greying hair worn in its usual plait, marred what was, surprisingly, given the druggy life she led, otherwise still a pretty face. 'He just sort of appeared in the yard one day and decided to stay. Our other dogs keep wanting to fight him so we're keeping him indoors till they get better acquainted.

'Hey, Crags, honey,' she called to the dog, 'come and make my Willow Tree's acquaintance.'

Aghast, Casey could only sit and stare in horror as the biggest, ugliest, dirtiest mongrel he had ever seen loped with a rangy stride over various outstretched bodies. Before Casey could do anything to stop him, the animal launched himself towards him, landed like dead weight in his lap and proceeding to rasp at his face with a huge and enthusiastic tongue.

Casey tried to hold him off as his nostrils were engulfed by the worst case of halitosis they'd ever encountered. Between rasps from a very rough tongue, Casey shouted furiously 'Get him off me!'

'Aw, don't be like that, Willow Tree,' Moon reproved. 'He's taken to you. I can tell.'

Thankfully, Moon called the dog over to her and to make up for Casey's unkind rejection, she made a big fuss of the Hound from Hell. The beast was more than big enough to make one believe that the dog who had 'appeared from nowhere', was a descendant of Black Shuck. He'd certainly brought death in his wake.

Now that the beast was no longer literally 'in his face', Casey could see the mutt's long-haired coat was heavily clogged with mud – and probably other things that Casey didn't want to think about. To his dismay, he saw that some of this mysterious muck had transferred itself to his previously immaculate suit and shirt.

Casey sighed. He shut his eyes. When he opened them again, it was to find Craggie gazing adoringly at him from huge, golden, crust-rimmed eyes. In case this latest member of the commune should take the eye contact as an invitation to launch another love-in, Casey hastily averted his gaze, though he had to admit that whilst undoubtedly smelly, Craggie was not even the most unhygienic commune member or the most averse to water; Star, Casey's father, won the ribbon on both counts.

'The dogs always bark at strangers,' his mother went on.

'Strangers on their own. We haven't been able to train them out of it.'

Only his parents would try to curb such a useful trait, he thought. Though, given the length of time any of their enthusiasms lasted, he doubted this 'training' had amounted to anything remotely likely to change the dogs' behaviour.

'But suppose it was a stranger who *wasn't* a stranger to the dogs? You said yourself that Craggie, for instance, just turned up one day and decided to stay.' Thinking of the commune's usual habits, he added, 'He looks, to me, the sort of ugly mutt that a drug dealer might favour for protection.'

Craggie whined at this and put one massive paw over his eyes.

'Now you've hurt his feelings,' Moon reproved again. 'Besides, you don't know him. Craggie's just an old softie, aren't you, boy?'

From beneath the filthy paw a deep 'woof' reverberated around the room.

'And do you really think we'd allow some drug dealer to roam around at will? We've kids here, Willow Tree, in case you hadn't noticed.' Striving for authentic indignation and failing, she added, 'We're not *that* irresponsible, you know.' This from a woman who had helped conceal one death and had doubtless considered concealing the second also.

If only her claim was true. But Casey knew that it wasn't. Neither Moon nor Star had hesitated when he was a kid to make their drug deals when he was around. They had dragged him halfway around India for months on the hippie trail of drugs and gurus, several times leaving him to fend for himself for days at a time while their attention was engaged by their latest wise man find. And, in his experience, their increasing years had made them no more responsible than they had ever been, as their current plight proved. In fact, sometimes, he thought they were getting worse – which he felt sure was something Rachel would tell him was an excellent reason to leave them to sort out their own problems this time.

Foxy Redfern used the pause in their exchange to enter

the commune's case for the defence. 'Whatever conclusions you two come to about Craggie and his fondness or otherwise for strangers, he and the other two dogs must have let *someone* in, man, without barking, as none of us had any reason to wish Kris ill.'

This brought another jangled chorus of agreement. It didn't convince Casey any more now than it had the last time and he made no attempt to conceal his scepticism. He had met the dead man briefly several times during his infrequent visits to his parents, and, though brief, the meetings had been enough to convince him that Kris Callender wasn't a man he could ever have liked. He also recalled hearing some muttered comments about Kris Callender, none of them complimentary.

'If all that you say about him is true, it strikes me as odd that you should decide to deny this divine being a decent burial and instead just unceremoniously dump him in an unhallowed hole in the ground.'

'It was less hassle, man,' Star, Casey's father, put in from where he was stretched out on the sofa. 'Besides—' he broke off and a puzzled look entered his eyes.

Casey guessed that, as was a frequent occurrence nowadays, his father had forgotten what else he had been going to say. Not for the first time in his relationship with his father, he forced himself to count to ten; at the end of this time, he managed, along with the look of reproof, to simply nod wearily.

Star subsided to his usual sloth after making his exhausting observation.

'Besides,' his mother broke in, 'we *didn't* bury him without any ceremony. We had candles and chanting and everything. Kris got a fabulous send-off.'

'And that's supposed to make it all right, is it?' Casey asked in a quiet voice.

One of the teenagers sprawled on one of the stained Indian rugs littering the new carpet sniggered.

From beneath black eyebrows, Casey fixed the youth with a stern green gaze. 'You think something about this is funny?' he asked the boy, a black-haired mid-teen who already sported heavy dark stubble. This growth was a recent addition; it certainly hadn't been evident on Casey's last visit and was so much the twin to Star's dark unshaven growth that Casey's eyes narrowed, the better to judge the boy's possible paternity. But then he decided he really didn't want to go there.

'Must I remind you that a man is dead?' He didn't add that a woman had also died. He had yet to question them about that. But he wanted to get the circumstances of the first death clear in his head before he started to question them about the second.

The youth – if he *had* sprung from Star's mostly indolent loins as Casey suspected – was certainly not a chip off Star's block and hadn't inherited his outlook, which was so slothfully laidback it was practically as horizontal as the man himself, for the boy defended himself with a vigour unknown to Casey's father.

'Kris "Krishna" Callender was a total tosser. Misnamed too; although he might have followed the womanizing aspect of Krishna's character, he sure as hell wasn't put on this earth to fight for good and combat evil like Lord Krishna. The man was evil.'

The youth directed a look of defiance at Casey, a defiance he proceeded to share around the room full of adults who tried to shush him.

But the youth wasn't to be silenced. 'I don't see why all of you seem so determined to pretend Kris was a great bloke and destined for sainthood. Because he was neither – ask my sister if you don't believe me,' he told Casey as he nodded to a very pregnant girl huddled in the far corner, who might – just – have scraped over the legal age of consent when she had conceived what, to judge from the youth's words, had to be the not-so-saintly Callender's baby.

'What's your name?' he asked the boy, having forgotten it.

'I'm Jethro Redfern and my sister's called Madonna.'

Casey nodded. Apt, he thought. For hadn't the original Madonna been impregnated by someone other than her husband? It was ironic that a group of people who chose to follow the sixties ethos of rebellion against the conventions of the previous austere decade and who had enthusiastically embraced such concepts as free love and taking drug-fuelled trips, should, in turn, themselves suffer from rebellious youth. But, as Casey noted from the set faces of the adults, the irony seemed to have escaped most of them.

Casey turned back to his mother. 'Is this true? Was Kris Callender such an unpleasant man?'

She didn't answer. Neither did anyone else.

Casey looked pointedly at Moon. 'Mum,' he said, 'you were the one who called me in. You were the one who asked me to pick up this poisoned chalice in order to help you all. How do you think I can do that if you won't tell me the truth?'

Casey's reasonable question brought only more silence.

'Fine,' he said as he stood up. 'Have it your own way. I'm out of here.' He turned towards the door, hoping to convince them that he was about to leave them to sort out their own mess. He hoped the shock of the two deaths and their current predicament had made his mother, at least, temporarily forget what a dutiful, responsible, totally unsuitable son he had turned into. But, in his heart, Casey knew he couldn't abandon them and as his mother let him know that she would cooperate he gave a brief sigh as he waved goodbye to that tiny window of opportunity when he might just have made his escape . . .

Instead, he sat down again to become yet another part of this guilty conspiracy of concealment.

'Jethro's right,' Moon now admitted. 'Kris wasn't a nice man. He was trouble almost from the day he arrived.'

'So why didn't you just kick him out?'

This reasonable question brought just a shrug of Moon's shoulders.

His father put in his second contribution of the evening. 'Kris had bad karma, man.'

After that, it didn't take Casey long to add to what he had already learned about Callender from young Jethro. Kris's 'bad karma' had basically consisted of most of the human vices of thieving, bullying, cheating and womanizing.

Jethro's sister wasn't the only young girl he had impregnated, Casey now discovered. Several girls in the neighbouring villages had also fallen victim to Callender's suspect charm; no wonder the commune members didn't get on with the locals. 'Free love', they called it. Yet, from where Casey was seated, the desolate look in young Madonna's eyes said that, for her at least, the 'love' she had shared with Callender had been far from cost free.

Now that he had forced them to tell him the truth about the first victim, he asked them about the second. 'This DaisyMay Smith – was she also disliked?'

'No, of course she wasn't,' Dylan Harper, her newly-bereaved partner, said sharply from the corner of his settee.

Dylan was a slim-hipped, gipsyish-looking man with springy dark curls and an array of golden earrings. At the moment, he looked as tautly sprung as his tight black curls. 'My Daisy was the most generous of women. She was also carrying our first child.' His voice broke on a sob as he added, 'And now I've lost her and the baby.'

'I'm sorry for your loss,' Casey told him gently.

Dylan Harper's emotional outburst contrasted strongly with the behaviour of Kris Callender's widow. Kali Callender's face looked the opposite of tear-stained even though her husband was dead and already in his makeshift grave. Though given what the others had to say about him, Mrs Callender's calm acceptance of her husband's death wasn't altogether surprising. Still, it was strange that she seemed to accept the very pregnant presence of her dead husband's much younger paramour. Most women would surely have found Madonna's continued presence intolerable.

Casey asked her, 'Did you know about your husband's secret burial? Did you *agree* to it?'

Kali Callender raised her chin a notch. Her gaze met his fearlessly – shamelessly, even.

'Yes,' she said. 'Of course I knew about it. I agreed to it. Kris was the worthless shit the others told you he was. The only honest day's work he's ever done was on our stall at the local market, and since we discovered that even that work wasn't honest at all, but just a means to cheat us all . . . I had no illusions about my husband.' She broke off, and in an echo of Jethro's youthful defiance, added, 'Hey, pig man, I was *glad* someone had killed him. I just wish whoever did it had done so sooner and saved me grief.'

Casey let her words die away before he again stood up. An uneasy communal sigh passed around the room. He assumed they feared that after Kali's insulting 'pig' reference, he was about to threaten to abandon them for a second time.

Reluctantly, only too aware of how deep in the mire he was already, he put them out of their misery.

'I'd like to see where you found Kris's body and where you buried him,' he told them. 'I also want to see the body of Ms Smith.'

The group all stood up, their expressions a mixture of relief, resignation and unease that even the cannabis-induced calm couldn't entirely eradicate. Led by Moon and Willow Tree Casey, they all trooped outside and made for Kris Callender's lonely grave. Casey was glad to get out into the fresh air, because the farmhouse smelled of a combination of unwashed dog, candle grease and the sweet, sickly odour of the cannabis that permeated the place. Partway there, and after tripping over he knew not what in the dark, Casey stopped them and suggested they would need a torch.

But as it seemed to be the general consensus that the commune didn't actually possess such a useful tool, they waited, huddled together against the chill night air while Casey walked back to his car, stepping carefully so as to avoid whatever other ready-to-trip-the-unwary rubbish the gloom might conceal, to retrieve his own torch from the boot.

The brief interruption in the grim night walk and the first solitary moments he'd had since his arrival gave Casey time to think. But as he considered the current situation and his part in it, he rather wished he hadn't. Because time to think tended only to increase his mental anguish, caused, not least, because if he hadn't suspected before he knew now that he wouldn't be able to trust even his parents to tell him the entire truth. Hadn't they already tried to mislead him about Callender's character?

Given this conclusion, for a few brief seconds, Casey was again tempted to abandon them and leave them to their fate. But just by making this one visit he had allowed himself to become too compromised to walk away. And although he liked to think that his parents wouldn't betray him unless it was when they were in a drugged-up, love-their-fellow-man, stupor, he had no illusions at all about the other members of the commune.

If one of them *had* murdered Kris Callender and DaisyMay Smith, which, given the presence of the barking dogs, seemed likely, and they thought he was getting close to the truth, they would surely shop him without question or hesitation in order to spread the burden of guilt.

Not for the first time, as he walked reluctantly back to the waiting group, Willow Tree Casey found himself envying the orphaned state of his DS, Thomas Catt.

Three

As they stood around the tumbled earth of the inexpertly dug grave, Casey questioned them all further and learned that – apart from his other assorted vices – Kris Callender had been a crack addict who had been found to be regularly exchanging a proportion of the commune's produce that he was supposed to sell at the local market to help support the community, for supplies of the drug to feed what had become an increasingly voracious habit.

It explained why Callender had been such a keen and dedicated stallholder, a realization which only amplified the indignation of the others.

But while Casey Callender's addiction added one more complication, to the commune members it meant only one thing – a let-off for them, for reasons they weren't slow to point out to Casey.

'We all thought it probable that Kris got on the wrong side of his dealer and was killed for his pains.' Foxy Redfern's enthusiasm for this explanation was such that he repeated it twice and then a third time with the slightest of alterations. 'If Kris *was* murdered, which none of us know for sure – for all we know he could have died from an over-dose – he must have been killed by an outsider rather than by a member of the commune.'

As they'd already been over this ground, Casey didn't comment. In the gloom beyond the range of the torch, he could see little more than the circle of white faces bobbing up and down as they again showed a ready willingness to support Foxy's theory. They seemed to have forgotten the 'barking dogs in the night time' at his arrival. Surely even their minimally retentive memories wouldn't allow them to forget the dogs' barking at strangers and have it both ways?

As they set off again, away from Kris Callender's hastily-dug grave, they walked towards an array of outbuildings at the back of the house. Seeking enlightenment, Casey asked, 'So why was it you decided to bury him rather than report his death? You still haven't told me.'

This time he got the answer that was, he judged, a deal closer to the truth than their earlier responses had been.

'We found his body here amongst our cannabis plants in one of the greenhouses,' Foxy Redfern told him, stopping so abruptly that Star cannoned into him.

It confirmed what Casey had suspected.

Foxy pointed through the open greenhouse door.

Casey, in the limited light the torch shed, hadn't recognized the plants.

'No way we wanted the cops here, poking their noses into our business. They'd have done us for sure. They're just looking for an opportunity. That crop brings us in bread, man. We didn't see why that shit, Kris, should bring us more grief when he was dead. He brought enough when he was alive.'

Some of the cannabis plants lay flattened on the soil, presumably where Callender's body had crushed them. Even these cash crops were surrounded by weeds, though here at least some attempt had been made to keep them in check.

'When did you find his body?' Casey asked, expecting the answer to be sometime in the last few days. DaisyMay Smith, the second victim, had been found only this morning and had still been warm to the touch, as his mother had told him on the phone. DaisyMay had clearly been but freshly killed. Casey thought it probable the two deaths were connected, so he was stunned at Foxy's reluctant admission.

'We found Kris's body two months ago.' He paused and frowned as he searched his drug-damaged memory. Then he conceded, 'Well, maybe it was a bit more than two months. I can't exactly recall.'

Clearly Foxy, helped by the light from the torch that

Casey still held, had noted the look of shocked dismay on Casey's face, for he added laconically, 'He'd have stayed in the ground, too, with no need to drag you into it, if it hadn't been for DaisyMay's death. You see that has definitely got to be murder. For, though in Kris's case the cause of his death was unclear, Daisy had obviously been beaten. Viciously beaten. It made us uneasy, man. Made us question who could have killed her. The thought that it might have been one of us unnerved the women. They persuaded Moon to phone you.'

'It wasn't just the women,' Dylan Harper insisted as his flashing gypsy dark eyes met Casey's. 'The "dead woman" as you keep calling her, was my *wife* – or at least the next best thing to it – we'd talked about getting married once the baby was born.'

Better late than never, was Casey's silent response to this.

'And even though she'll still end up in a hole in the ground, I wanted my wife to be properly buried, to have an *official* hole in the ground instead of a hole in the corner such as we dug for Callender. My Daisy's entitled to a proper burial and I insisted she got one. *That's* the main reason Moon rang you. Even though the women were spooked, they'd have been persuaded to get over it but for my insistence.'

Star butted in. 'Hey man,' he said, 'that doesn't vibe with my memory.'

With a degree of contempt evident in his voice, Dylan Harper said, 'No. But then you rarely ever recall anything as it really was, do you?' He sighed, and ignoring Star, he stared down at the crushed cannabis plants and added, 'The rest you know,' before he turned away.

This situation just got better and better, Casey thought as, from Kris's place of death, they made for the outhouse where DaisyMay's body currently lay. Casey made them all remain outside. Although if the worst happened and Casey's relationship to Moon and Star was discovered by the local police and thence conveyed to his own force, any stray DNA that he left in the house could be explained by his visits over the years, any found in the shed could not be so easily explained away, so he insisted, in spite of the 'Hey, man' protests, on donning a set of the protective gear that he had brought from the car before he entered the shed. As he said to himself, any reasonably competent investigating officer from the local force would be likely to wonder at finding traces of another, unknown set of DNA in one of the commune's outhouses. They would then spread their net wide, which would certainly include *him* once they found out the connection, even if it was simply for elimination purposes.

He was risking his career enough just by *being* here. But trying to help his parents and the others was an entirely different matter. There was no point in needlessly increasing the dangers to himself by being as careless as the rest.

But as Foxy Redfern had pointed out, they were as yet uncertain if the dead man had even been murdered. He might well have just died from natural causes or an overdose of the unnatural substances with which he had regularly abused his body.

Foxy Redfern had been right when he had said that DaisyMay Smith had been viciously beaten, as Casey saw when he lifted the sheet that covered her body and shone his torch at her.

She lay on a board propped on a couple of trestles in one of the sheds that had been turned into a makeshift morgue. Someone had surrounded her body with candles – worn down to half-used stubs by now. Their yellow flames gave the dead woman's face a healthy glow that was unnatural and so eerie, Casey felt the hairs on the back of his neck stand up.

And as he played the torch over her and stared down at her poor, marked face that, for all the lifelike colour the candles gave it, was clearly no longer of *this* world, Casey saw that one of the bones in her right arm looked misshapen. Presumably, it had been broken during the frenzied assault while DaisyMay had tried to defend herself.

His examination of the body by the torch and candlelight made clear it had been moved after death, the dark post-mortem hypostasis made that self-evident, without the need for further corroboration, but Casey decided this was a case that needed all the corroboration it could get, given its location and his involvement.

'So, where did you find DaisyMay's body? And when was she last seen?'

'She was last seen by Madonna in the kitchen around ten-ish this morning,' Moon replied. 'No one else remembers seeing her after that.'

Casey wasn't surprised at this. Which of them, apart from the young and naïve Madonna, would be foolish enough to admit to being the last to see DaisyMay alive?

'She was found in the apple orchard,' his mother, Moon, explained. 'Lord Krishna knows what she was doing there as the apples aren't yet ready for harvesting. It's a good distance from the house and as there are several more outhouses between the orchard and the house the noise of any cries would have been muffled.'

Casey nodded. After he let the sheet fall back over DaisyMay's poor battered face he shone his torch on his watch. It was late. Rachel would certainly have returned home from her theatre trip by now. In his haste, he had forgotten to leave a note to explain his absence. Not wishing to be disturbed while he questioned his parents and the rest, he had switched his mobile off. But now, as he ushered them all ahead of him as he left the shed and followed behind them, leaving DaisyMay Smith and her encircling candle stubs alone again, he switched it on and gave Rachel a quick, reassuring call.

'Hi, sweetheart,' he said quietly for Rachel's ear alone. 'Sorry I didn't leave you a note. I got an urgent call-out.' More loudly, for the benefit of his fellow conspirators as well as Rachel, he added the rider, 'I'll tell you all about it when I get home.'

As he returned the mobile to his pocket, Casey faced the commune members and said, 'As you'll tell the local police all about it tonight as soon as I've gone.'

They seemed to be surprised by this instruction and a noisy hubbub of protests broke out.

What had they expected? Casey wondered grimly. That

he'd be as keen as most of them had been to sweep two deaths under some convenient soil carpet, solve the murders himself in the space of an hour or so and leave them to go about their business as if the deaths had never happened?

But while he marvelled at such an expectation, he thought it probable that was just what they *had* expected. It would be in keeping with their general laissez faire attitude.

Determinedly, Casey set about destroying any such lingering hopes. It took about ten minutes before their drug- and death-dazed brains managed to take in that he meant what he said. But at least by the time he was finished, he concluded from their silence that they had conceded they had no choice but to contact the police and formally report the two deaths.

Casey decided to leave it up to them to figure out what answer they came up with to explain the fact that Kris 'Krishna' Callender had been in his grave for two months or more without benefit of either death certificate or coroner's inquest. He didn't envy them the task.

Before he drove off, Casey raked his lights over the front of the farmhouse, first full beam, then dipped, then full beam again, as a reminder to them that although *he* might be going away, their problems certainly wouldn't. He had told them it would look better if they did as he had force-fully suggested and report the two deaths themselves, rather than leaving him to make good their failure to do so, which was something he had promised them he would do if he had to. From their sullen expressions as he had climbed in the car, Casey knew they believed him.

Of course, it was a threat that he was loath to carry out. He hadn't spent years making sure that the reality of his parental inheritance didn't damage his career to step volun-tarily into the limelight of a murder investigation now and announce to the world that the commune had called him in because he was the policeman son of two of the drug-taking hippie suspects.

Fortunately, he believed they were all even more dazed

by the day's events than they usually were by drugs, and therefore incapable of the coherent thought necessary for such a conclusion.

But even if the various commune members failed to grasp this fact, Casey was aware that it was only by staying in the background and organizing an unofficial, behind the scenes investigation away from the commune that he would both keep his career free from contamination and attempt to find the killer and help his parents and the rest out of their predicament. Casey reflected on the damage that would be done to his career should it come out that the commune had called him in the belief that he would help them conceal the deaths. As it was, he had been persuaded not to reveal his relationship to the police. He hadn't taken much persuading. Besides, as Moon had pointed out, 'Willow Tree, hon, the only way we'll get a fair hearing is if *you* look into the deaths. I realize you can't do it officially, but at least when the official pigs turn up and arrest us all you'll be able to find the evidence that we didn't kill our friends.'

As he drove back to King's Langley and its comparative sanity, Casey wished he could be sure on that point. Bemused, he stared through the still lingering mist on the road as he pondered how his mother expected him to come up with the goods, given that what the commune members had so far told him had been little enough and that a mixture of truth and lies, the little made less owing to the hazy memories of the long-term drug user.

He only hoped, with the smallholding about to be overrun by the forces of Lincolnshire's finest, that no member of the commune either deliberately betrayed him for newspaper money or accidentally let slip his identity or his unofficial, unreported actions of the last few hours.

It was after he arrived home but before he had a chance to make his own shamefaced confession about his recent activities that Rachel exclaimed at the state of his new suit.

At her look of horror, Casey looked down and saw she had reason for her exclamation. His new suit was ruined. Between getting caught on rusty wire that had ripped it in several places, coming into contact with deep, noxious puddles in the yard and suffering Craggie's mud-covered and drooling embrace, the suit was surely beyond salvage. Besides, Casey didn't think he would ever want to wear it again as it would never feel *clean* again.

It was £500 down the drain, because he thought it unlikely he would be up to brazening out the insurance claim form and its inquisitorial demands as to how, where and when the suit had sustained such damage.

As expected, after he had told Rachel about his nocturnal activities, she told him what he already knew – that it hadn't been only his parents and the rest who had behaved foolishly. By taking their problems on to his own shoulders, he had shown himself to be the biggest fool of all. Worse, he knew she was right.

'You realize you could lose your career over this if it comes out?' she asked.

Casey nodded miserably, a misery only exacerbated as she added a rider.

'Or worse.'

Because he knew she was right about that as well. Only, somehow, he'd not been able to leave his parents, Moon and Star, to deal with their own failure of morality and responsibility. He never had been able to. But maybe, if by some miracle he came through this current problem without a stain on his character or career, he might start to think differently in future.

As Rachel said before she stumped off to bed, maybe it was time he did.

Four

As expected, by the next morning, the story of the two smallholding deaths had surfaced. Casey had gone out early to learn the worst and as he scanned the shelves of the nearest newsagent, he saw that they featured as front page news in all the local newspapers as well as several of the nationals. He bought a selection and carried them home to read them more thoroughly and see if his name had escaped into the public domain.

As he sipped his breakfast coffee and quickly searched the lines of newsprint opposite a silently reproachful Rachel, he just hoped no one who knew both him *and* his parents decided to inform the papers of their relationship. At least, so far, his secret was holding up.

He had, of course, taken considerable trouble throughout his police career to keep an identity distance from his parents, aware that if the connection came out it would do his career no good at all. So far – apart from in one instance – it had worked well. But that one instance had involved his sergeant, so Casey wasn't altogether surprised when DS Thomas Catt rang his mobile shortly after.

'Hey, Willow Tree,' ThomCatt greeted him, chafing him by using Casey's given name instead of the 'Will' which he had taken care was the name by which he was commonly known.

It told Casey that Catt, too, had read the morning's papers.

'Please don't tell me you're the same Casey whose parents are front page news this morning.'

'I wish I didn't have to, ThomCatt,' Casey admitted. 'Unfortunately, I *am* that very same Casey.'

Tom's piercing whistle caused Casey to hold his mobile

away from his ear with a grimace of pain. When he returned
the phone to his ear, it was to hear Tom say, 'I presume
you know all about it?'

After Rachel's reaction, Casey was unwilling to make a
second admission about his nocturnal activities – unwilling,
at first, even to confirm Tom's guess.

But ThomCatt, whose nickname had in part been
bestowed because he shared the feline's cussed single-
minded curiosity, wasn't to be put off.

'Come off it, Will. We both know you're the patsy your
parents turn to at the first whiff of trouble. It's inconceivable to me that they wouldn't have called you in to sort out
this latest bit of bother, especially with you being on holiday
and with time on your hands.'

Last night had proved that it had been inconceivable to
his parents as well, reflected a more than rueful Casey.
Reluctantly, as he accepted that Tom's logical assessment
was unassailable, he admitted, 'OK. Yes, they did call me
in. But keep it under your hat.'

Tom whistled again.

'Will you stop doing that?' Casey asked irritably. Understandably, his normally calm demeanour had deserted him.

'Sorry. But I want to help. So what's on the agenda?'

'For you, work. You've got a job to do, remember? As
you pointed out, *I'm* currently on holiday. Besides, I don't
see what you can do all the way down here in Norfolk,
especially when you're doing the usual full shift.'

Both men were based in King's Langley, a small market
town of medieval origins in Norfolk that was situated
midway between Peterborough and Norwich – a good way
from Casey's parents' Fenland smallholding, which was this
side of Boston on the east coast.

'I don't see what you can do, either – officially,' Tom
retorted with his usual respect-for-authority failure, 'seeing
as you can hardly poke your nose into the Lincolnshire
investigation. I suppose you've already questioned your
parents and the other commune members?'

'Last night.'

'And?'

Casey explained what he had learned the previous night. He was just about to remove the phone from his ear again in anticipation of another piercing whistle, but Tom must have thought better of it.

'You're going to need help, Will,' his DS insisted. 'Checking everyone's motives and opportunities, not to mention finding out the identity of the dead man's supplier while keeping out of the way of the official investigation is not going to be easy. Certainly, it's not a one-man job. For a kick off *I've* got one or two contacts up that way, but as I'd guess you keep a low profile when visiting your parents, I very much doubt that you have. Am I right?'

Casey made another reluctant admission. Catt *was* right, of course, Understandably, he'd always done his best to keep the low profile ThomCatt had referred to on his infrequent visits to his parents. He had also kept these visits as short as duty permitted, without trips to the pub with the casual and nosy acquaintances such trips struck up.

'So – do you want me to call these contacts and see if they can suss out the ID of Callender's drug supplier?'

Thomas Catt invariably had 'contacts' all over the place. Many of them were retained from the youth spent in assorted children's homes when he had made some unlikely friendships – not all of them either unsavoury or without contacts of their own.

Grateful that ThomCatt had so willingly offered his services, Casey felt unable to do anything but agree, only too aware that he wasn't in a position to refuse such generously offered assistance.

'But keep as low a profile as if you were me visiting Moon and Star at the commune, Tom,' he warned. 'They're my parents, so it's only right that my career should be put in jeopardy for their sakes. There's no reason why the same need apply to yours.'

'Keep cool, Big Willy,' Catt advised cockily. 'And don't worry. Ain't I a big boy now?' Casey imagined him patting the beginnings of a paunch as Catt added, 'And getting bigger all the time. Besides, I've always preferred my life to be enlivened with a little spice. I can take some of the load and keep a low profile at the same time. Smart as paint, me,' he boasted with the confidence of a cheeky Cockney sparrow that Casey could, at the moment, only envy.

Casey hoped – for Tom's sake – that his boast – and his confidence – didn't prove misplaced.

From what the newspapers said, it hadn't taken the Lincolnshire police long to charge all the adults at the commune with the less serious crimes of failing to report Kris's death, of burying his body without official sanction and growing cannabis with intent to supply. Further, greater charges were likely to follow unless Casey, with Catt's help, could come up trumps.

Because as the papers Casey had so feverishly scanned earlier had speculated with their usual careful libel avoidance while still making their comments perfectly comprehensible, after the commune's unorthodox behaviour, they might well soon face further charges of a much more serious nature.

Aware immediately after he had spoken to Moon but prior to his surreptitious trip to the Fens the previous night, that it would be impossible in the near future with the police on site to again visit the commune, the top of whose lane was, as expected, this morning besieged by the usual press pack, Casey had stopped off on the way to the Fens and bought a new pay-as-you-go mobile. He had handed it to his mother with the instruction 'Please don't lose this one.'

Anticipating the arrests and the listing of their possessions by the custody sergeant, Casey had also instructed her to conceal the mobile somewhere as secure as she could find on the smallholding in anticipation of their release on police bail. He had also instructed her to make sure the cannabis growing in one of the commune greenhouses was dug up and destroyed. The newspaper reports made clear the latter instruction had been ignored and he had little confidence his instructions about the mobile would have been noted and acted upon either. But he could only do so much. If Moon, Star and the rest chose not to cooperate there was little or nothing he could do about it.

He made another coffee and sipped it slowly. He just had to hope she had obeyed his first injunction, for he would need to be able to contact her regularly. He had told her that, once they were released on bail, he would ring her every evening around seven o'clock.

Meanwhile, he had instructed, she was to search her unfortunately drug-raddled memory for any clues as to who might have been responsible for the murder of DaisyMay Smith and the probable murder of Kris Callender. He wanted means, motives and opportunities, he had told her, 'And you're the only one I can rely on to get them for me.' And he wasn't too sure about *her*. He had good reason to doubt after such an interval that she would remember much more about Callender's death than she had already told him. Casey had already discounted the possibility of getting any useful help from his father. Sloth-like, Star ambled his way through life, noticing little or nothing, besides which, his memory was notoriously poor and he had difficulty stringing half a dozen words together before his brain faltered to a standstill. He would have enough trouble coming up with an alibi for himself even for DaisyMay Smith's very recent murder, or of providing clues as to which of his fellow commune members might be guilty of such violence, never mind demanding answers of his memory about Kris Callender's death which had occurred two months or more ago.

As for the drug supplier they had mentioned, he would have to leave identifying him to ThomCatt because, although he had questioned each of the commune about the supplier's identity, they had all denied knowing anything about him. A denial that Casey didn't for a moment believe.

He assumed they were scared that if this dealer thought they had reported him to the police he might well decide to do to them what, in their insistence on their own innocence, they were determined to believe he had already done to Kris Callender and DaisyMay Smith. Though if this unknown outsider *had* killed Callender, it didn't explain why DaisyMay was the only one of the two who had been *brutally* murdered. She rarely left the confines of the commune these days, Moon had told him, and unless this dealer was the more obliging sort who went in for home deliveries, it was unlikely she had had anything to do with him or any other dealers. Besides, since her pregnancy, which was apparently a troublesome one which left her rarely feeling well, DaisyMay had given up drug-taking so was unlikely to require the services of a dealer.

Fortunately, Casey had been able to obtain, for his parents at least if not the rest, the services of an excellent solicitor and they had both been released on bail this morning pending further inquiries.

Casey was more wary than ever with the police probably still on site, and even though he had put her new mobile on a non-ringing setting, he was reluctant to call his mother at their appointed time that evening. Instead, he texted her and told her to ring him back but to find somewhere well out of police earshot before she did so.

Rather to Casey's surprise, she obeyed the instruction and rang five minutes later, clearly rattled by the invading presence of so many 'pigs' on the commune's smallholding.

'You've got to help us, Willow Tree,' she told him with a trace of what sounded like hysteria evident in her normally laidback voice. 'You know how little brotherly love the local pigs have for us.'

Casey suspected his mother was right about that. The commune's presence on the edge of the village was not liked by the neighbours, who not unreasonably thought that with their irresponsible, druggy lifestyles they attracted other undesirables. The local police had a down on them for a similar reason.

Casey thought it unlikely the local Lincolnshire constabulary would be able to pass up the temptation to get the whole lot of them out of their hair completely and permanently, by charging them with murder before, during and after the fact. And given the commune members' behaviour up to press, it wasn't unreasonable that DCI Boxham, the man in charge of the Fenland investigation, should feel confident of success.

After all, they had buried Kris Callender – an indicator of guilt if ever there was one. And if the post-mortem on his remains proved conclusively that he *had* been murdered, their defence, already questionable and faintly surreal, would quickly become farcical. Not to mention unsustainable.

God knew that Moon, Star and the rest of their raggle-taggle band of brothers, sisters and kids of as many colours as Joseph's Amazing Technicolor Dreamcoat wouldn't have endeared themselves to the investigating officers by firstly burying Kris without making any attempt to report his death and then by leaving it till hours after they had found DaisyMay's body to actually contact the police. The fact that she appeared to have been brutally beaten to death would, for Boxham and his team, make this delay even more reprehensible.

Casey, listening intently as Moon poured out the details of what the local force had so far said and done, recognized that he'd been backed into a corner from which the only escape would be to find a solution to the deaths that would prove his parents' innocence. He knew it would be a far from easy, maybe an impossible, task.

'So, what did you find out, Thomas?' Casey asked the following morning, with an unconscious formality as he opened the front door of his home and ushered Catt inside.

'Thomas? Oh, dear. Have I been a naughty boy, then, to get my full moniker?'

'What?' For a moment, Casey had no idea what his DS was talking about. Then he realized and apologized for his distant manner. Casey supposed that it was only by adopting a formal air – even unconsciously – that he felt he had any control left at all.

'That's all right. Stress takes us all in different ways. Rachel in?' Catt cautiously enquired before he ventured any deeper into the house.

Casey shook his head. 'She's gone shopping with a girl-friend to take her mind off my predicament,' he told Catt. He wished the retail therapy of replacing his ruined suit could take *his* mind from his current seemingly insurmountable problems. But as there was no hope of that, he made coffee and they retreated to the living room to work on their unofficial murder inquiry.

Once settled in the living room, a large, tidy room with many books and neat piles of musical scores, which, unlike his parents' home, boasted no clutter, mugs in hand – a small tot of vodka enlivening Catt's coffee – Casey began to question him again.

'One of my contacts has been in touch,' Catt told him. 'He's talked to various people, some druggy and keen to remain friends with their supplier and some non-druggy and with no need to keep on the guy's right side. By the way, Callender's crack dealer is a bloke called Tony Magann. The usual nasty piece of work, so my sources tell me.'

Catt paused, took a sip of vodka-laced coffee. 'There's no way of knowing exactly when that guy, Kris Callender, died, you said?'

'No. All the commune could tell me was that it was around two months ago.'

Casey didn't add that nothing the commune members had told him could be taken as gospel. Besides, Catt was smart as a whip apart from being as familiar with the effects of long-term drug use as he was himself, so would be able to come to the inevitable conclusion.

'OK,' he said, 'I get the drift.' Proving to Casey that his own conclusion had been tellingly accurate. 'For the dead bloke, two months is the – very rough – timescale. Understood. But for the girl, we've got a reasonably accurate time of death, you said?'

Casey confirmed it. 'The timescale's about three to four hours. DaisyMay Smith was last seen around ten a.m. in the kitchen of the smallholding. Apparently, she and Madonna Redfern were comparing notes on their pregnancies and arguing as to who was having the worst time. She was found dead in the apple orchard behind the farmhouse around two o'clock that same afternoon.'

'Then this drug dealer bloke Magann can't have killed her,' Catt told him. 'He was, according to all sources I spoke to, including the hospital, visiting his sick mother from ten in the morning till after four that day.'

Appalled at the news that he had lost such a strong suspect so early in their shadowing investigation and even though the evidence of the dogs made the scenario of the drug dealer as the killer unlikely, wishful thinking was hard to eradicate. Casey could only stare at his sergeant in horror. 'Don't tell me that,' he pleaded.

'Sorry, boss. But even drug dealers can have mothers they love,' Catt remarked, dryly. 'And Magann is very, very sick. Practically at death's door according to the hospital. No,' Catt told him decisively, 'he can't have done that one, at least. And as you're convinced the two deaths must be connected in some way, it doesn't seem likely that he could have had anything to do with the first one, either.

'So, unless we or the official investigating officers can discover some other criminally-minded outsider who had dealings with one or more of the commune, had ready access to the place and was familiar to the dogs, we're stuffed.'

Catt didn't need to add – 'And so are your parents and the rest.'

This news brought Casey – and his unofficial invest-igation – squarely and inescapably, back, for his chief suspects, to the members of the commune. It didn't help that all of them had criminal records, as Tom didn't fail to remind him.

'So much for the "Summer of Love" generation and their adherents,' ThomCatt quipped. 'It seems they're as keen on cheating, lying and stealing as much of the rest of humanity. More it seems, in Callender's case.

'I told you, luckily for us, I've got a friend on the Lincolnshire force that's dealing with the commune killings and who owes me a huge favour so I have pretty much ready access to their discoveries.'

That was the one piece of good news Casey had heard since Moon had first telephoned. He, of course, already knew most of the commune's more grubby details. As ThomCatt had said, this loving brother and sisterhood did their fair share of wrong-doing, whether it was coveting their neighbours' asses or their wives and daughters. Certainly, a fair bit of the latter had been going on there, as Madonna Redfern's advanced pregnancy alone could testify.

Of course, all of them had drug convictions and now Tom told him that Foxy Redfern also had a very recent conviction for drunken assault and Kali Callender had one charge of soliciting against her, though it *was* several years back. At least Tom was sensitive enough not to mention Casey's parents' convictions.

Casey consoled himself with the thought that at least none of them had records for GBH or worse. He disliked being dependent for all his information on Catt's favour-owing and possibly more than dodgy friend, but he dare not consult the police national computer himself. He had no official involvement in the case, so was unwilling to leave his technological fingerprints all over it.

You never knew when such prints might come back and point the finger. He had cautioned Catt similarly. Not that he'd needed to, as Catt, who had spent nearly all his child-hood in council-run care homes, had grown wily at an early age in order to survive his upbringing. He knew better than to leave fingerprint or any other traces of himself behind.

'Was your mother able to pin down the whereabouts of the other commune members between the times DaisyMay Smith was last seen and when her body was found?'

Casey shook his head. 'Not really. Bits and pieces, that's all, which means that any one of them could have killed her.' Including Moon and Star themselves, he reluctantly acknowledged. And although Casey had little doubt that Star was too idle to exert himself to so violently attack anybody, his mother had always been the more determined and energetic of the two – which wasn't saying a lot, of course, but even so . . .

He took a gulp of his coffee, wishing now that he had laced it with spirits as he had Catt's and comforted himself with the thought that as far as he knew, Moon had no reason to kill either Kris Callender or DaisyMay Smith. Unless she had discovered that Star, her idle husband, had suddenly developed a new lease of life in the love-making department and had impregnated DaisyMay?

But that was another area Casey was reluctant to investigate too closely. He ran his hand through his neatly cut black hair and said, 'OK. So what about the other death?'

Keen as mustard, cheerfully, Tom said, 'It's my understanding that these hippie communes tend to attract transient types who prefer to pick up their sticks and little spotted handkerchiefs and take off after a while in one place. Were all the current inhabitants there when Callender's body was found?'

Casey thought back over what his mother had told him. Then he nodded. 'But there was also another couple staying there around that time. Names of Honey and Ché Farrer. I remembered them and asked Moon about them.'

'What reason did they give for leaving?'

'According to Moon, they couldn't get on with Callender.'

'I presume he was still alive after this Farrer pair left?'

'Debatable.' From somewhere, Casey managed to find a wry smile. It felt unnaturally forced. 'Moon can't remember. She knows the two events were close together, but she's unclear in which order they occurred. She takes drugs, used to take a lot of them. Regularly,' he spelled out to the already clued-up Catt. 'She's asked the others, of course. Most of them can't remember, either. And the ones who said they can, according to Moon, gave off a distinct whiff of wanting to spread the collective guilt as widely as possible.'

'You've primed her to mention this Farrer couple to the investigating coppers?'

'Of course. And to avoid the distinct possibility that she'll forget all about them by the time she next sees DCI Boxham, I told her she might consider getting a bit of exercise and walking the half-mile into the village to telephone him from the public phone box. No way do I want her contacting DCI Boxham from the secret mobile. If he gets its number, he might just think to track down her other calls.'

Casey had felt he had to tell Catt about this after he'd done so much to help. His warning to Moon about using this mobile for such a call had been emphatic. If it occurred to Boxham to trace her call back to their sole means of communication it would put paid to any hope that Casey had that he would be able to remove his parents' names from the list of murder suspects.

That this mobile was the only means of communication between himself and his parents was another anxiety to Casey. Because, as he confided to Catt, it could surely only be a matter of time before Moon either forgot where she'd hidden it or, as had happened to the previous mobiles he'd bought his parents, lost it altogether.

'She could always take up smoke signalling,' Catt joked.

But while aspects of this case might amuse ThomCatt, Casey couldn't afford such levity. As he said, 'With the number of smoke signals her and Star's illicit substances have sent up over the years, I'd rather my parents stayed away from such things. With his local knowledge and his familiarity with the commune and their ways, Boxham would be only too likely to read such signals. And then where would we be?'

'Mm. So what now? Do you want me to put the word out that we'd like to trace this Farrer couple?'

'No. Let the official team do that. You'd have to spread the word way too widely to find them as they could be anywhere in the country. Maybe even abroad by now. Leave it to the Lincolnshire force.' Casey hesitated, then, because it was so important, found himself breathlessly – anxiously – asking, 'Your contact there isn't beginning to fight shy of sharing further information, I hope? Because without his input we're likely to flounder.'

'No,' Catt reassured in his best breezy manner. 'He's fine. Besides, he used to be a bit of a hippie himself in his younger days, did the whole bit – the travelling around India; the meditating; the drugs . . . Anyway, he loathes DCI Boxham, so would be only too pleased to help us prove his determination to pin these deaths on one or other of the commune members is wrongheaded and probably, nowadays, politically incorrect as well.'

Catt drained the rest of his vodka-laced coffee, rose, clapped a consoling hand on Casey's shoulder and said,

'I've got to get back to work. I'll keep you posted on what I hear from my various sources. And stop worrying. I can't see either of your parents murdering anybody.'

Casey nodded and let Tom out, watching as he made his carefree way down the path and out of the gate. He just wished DCI Boxham proved equally as magnanimous on the subject. But, for the life of him and as hard as he tried, he didn't think it at all likely.

Five

After Thomas Catt had left, Casey made himself some more coffee and settled down to write up some notes while events were still fresh in his mind until Rachel should deign to return and he was obliged to make an effort to pretend to be interested in continuing with their much looked-forward to holiday. Various days and half-days out had been planned which he felt unable to get out of.

Even though they had a habit of periodically going off on trips, he had known all of the more long-standing members of his parents' commune for a number of years. Now he set about recalling as much as he could about them all.

Kali Callender, the tear-free widow of the late Kris, had struck him on the few occasions he'd encountered her as being almost as unpleasant a character as her dead husband was reputed to be. Not for nothing had she been nicknamed for the Hindu goddess Kali, known as 'the Black One', one of the most fearsome of the vast array of pleasant and not so pleasant Hindu deities which he had learned about during his parents' hippie treks around India in his childhood and youth. As Kali Callender had metaphorically done to her husband, the goddess Kali was most often depicted dancing on the 'corpse' of Shiva while garlanded with a tasteful array of human heads. *Not* a goddess the more pacifically-minded Casey would be willing to bow down and worship, particularly as her bloodlust for war and carnage had, until it was outlawed in the early nineteenth century, only been appeased by human sacrifice of the more brutal kind. Had Kali sacrificed her husband and DaisyMay from some vengeful bloodlust which only she knew the reason for? He hoped not as he suspected the widow the most likely of the bunch to be able to keep her own counsel.

Certainly, as Moon had reluctantly confided, the widow Callender had an unfortunate tendency to argue, which trait, owing to having to live so closely with the others in the commune who all had drug habits of various extents and expense and who could also be as argumentative and selfish as she was herself, would tend to exacerbate. There was a definite possibility that Mrs Callender herself had decided to 'off' her husband, tiring of waiting for one of the others to lose their drug-addled heads sufficiently to do it for her.

As for the rest and their possible motives, Glen 'Foxy' Redfern, he of the belligerent manner and the fiery frizz of bright red hair, had shown himself as the most eager for the blame for the murders to be laid on an outsider. Whether he was hoping to conceal his own guilt by blaming an outsider was unclear, though the rest, probably just as eager for any blame to be apportioned elsewhere, had backed him up quickly enough. Then there was Foxy's wife, Lilith, and their son Jethro; strangely, it had been Jethro, Madonna's older brother, who had seemed most cut up about her early pregnancy. Not that Casey could hold that against the youngster, who would perhaps blame his parents for his sister's situation almost as much as he had blamed Callender himself.

That their parents had chosen to rear their children in an atmosphere of sleaze and moral bankruptcy didn't mean their teenage offspring would necessarily find such an atmosphere appealing. Witness Saffron in *Absolutely Fabulous*, who had certainly not approved of *her* maternal parent's lifestyle and who lived her life in as opposite a manner to it as she could.

Much like me with my parents, Casey thought as he recalled the necessity of keeping himself fed whilst in India with the pair, after his parents had abandoned him while they sought the wisdom of yet another guru. He'd been all of ten that first time. And although feeling frightened and alone, he'd managed, necessity being the mother of invention.

All three of the Redferns might well have felt antagonistic

towards Callender for impregnating the teenage Madonna, as well might Madonna Redfern herself.

Certainly Madonna had looked miserable enough about the situation in which she currently found herself. And as for Jethro, perhaps for all that he seemed familiar with the Indian culture that had so absorbed the older generation in their youth and presumably still did, perhaps, like Casey himself, he had merely absorbed it in much the same way as one does language or anything else that surrounds one every day and it meant no more to him than that.

As for Dylan Harper, the other bereaved commune member, Casey considered the short of stature gipsy-dark man. Like a lot of smaller men, Dylan appeared to hold a lot of anger in his slim frame. An anger that seemed to Casey all too likely to explode if he felt he had reason to believe one of the other commune members had killed his partner. If he suspected he knew the guilty party, he might well take a violent, gipsy revenge – a murder waiting to happen. He just hoped Moon and Star weren't on Harper's list of potential suspects.

Casey had warned Moon to stay away from him as much as possible, certainly not to provoke him in any way.

Scott 'Mackenzie' Johnson and Randy Matthews, his much younger lover, had said little during Casey's last visit. Both were relative newcomers to the commune: Scott had moved in first, with his partner, Randy, whom he had met some time after, moving in only six months previously. Their failure to voice any opinion about the deaths struck Casey as odd. Such deliberate low profiles might indicate that they were intent on concealing something.

But then, he realized they had said little during his previous visits either, though in Randy's case at least, he hadn't been there for most of them, having only taken up with Scott Johnson some six months earlier. He was the newcomer in an established set-up and was probably still feeling his way.

It was around lunchtime, just before Rachel returned from her therapeutic shopping trip, when Catt rang.

'I've just learned the results of the two post-mortems,' he told Casey. 'Hang on to your hat.'

'Go on. It's not as if I haven't been expecting the worst.'

'That's all right, then. So you're not going to be disappointed. Much as we expected, both Kris Callender *and* DaisyMay Smith were murdered. Callender died from a blow to the head with the proverbial blunt instrument. So did Ms Smith, for that matter, though Callender didn't endure the assault she sustained before death. As in Callender's case, the blows caused a cerebral haemorrhage.'

Although the cause of death was the same in each case, which in such an enclosed location would usually indicate the same murderer, the two killings were completely different in other ways. As ThomCatt had said, the killing of poor DaisyMay had been a far more brutal one. There had been real savagery there. Was it really possible that one or more of the so-called peace-loving members of the commune could be guilty of such violence? But, he told himself, of course they could. They were an argumentative lot. It was but a small step from arguing to physical violence as the many knife murders in modern society made clear.

'So, what's DCI Boxham's thinking on the case?' Casey asked.

'He's being very cagey,' Catt reported. 'My source was able to tell me little of his boss's thoughts. As to the plan, I gather that is to continue their questioning of the commune members until one of them loses their nerve and blurts out the truth, though I could have told him that. I gather the questioning has been pretty relentless since the investigation began.'

Casey hadn't expected anything else. He wondered how they were all standing up to it. He thought Moon would hold up pretty well. He just wished he could say the same about his father. Star would find such relentless questioning difficult, particularly as he would be deprived of the several regular daytime naps he was used to and – given his general inability to complete a sentence – was unlikely to be able to answer most of the questions anyway, which would only

incline the officers assigned to his questioning to increase
the pace still further.

Casey stifled a worried sigh. 'Thanks for letting me know,
Tom.'

'I just wish I had better news for you. Still, look on the
bright side, hey? They haven't yet charged anyone with
murder.'

'True.'

But as he thanked Tom again and put the phone down,
Casey reflected that that was surely likely to be only a
matter of time.

Meanwhile, he would badger his memory and carry on
with noting down all that he knew about each of the
commune members. Firstly, it was clear that the commune
smallholding was far from being a latter-day Sunnybrook
Farm. The discovery of Callender's treachery over the
sale of their limited and ill-cared-for produce had clearly
caused a lot of bad feeling. The Redferns, because of
Madonna's teenage pregnancy, all had reason to wish
Callender ill, as, presumably, judging from her caustic
comments, did Kali, his wife. And to judge from what
Jethro Redfern had said, none of the rest of the commune
had reason to love the man either, though again, their
dislike – hatred, even – of Callender didn't explain
DaisyMay's murder. Her death was something of a conundrum. But Callender's death at least was easily explained.
In fostering hatred amongst the rest it seemed probable
he had brought about his own death. From the little Moon
had let escape and from what he had observed, it
had become evident that the commune was a hotbed of
hatreds and partisanships rather than the Utopia of popular
imagination.

Young Jethro, for one, apart from holding the adults in
low esteem, had been vociferous in his contempt for the
dead man. Had that been simply the cry of outspoken and
foolish youth? Or was he canny enough to speak of his
dislike of Callender as a form of double bluff? Did he
believe that his very outspokenness would render the police
– and Casey himself – less likely to consider him a major

suspect? It was possible; he was young enough to try such a bluff, unaware that the police had plenty of experience of such tactics.

So far, Casey had reduced the motives to three possibilities: that Callender had been killed by one or more of the commune because they had found out about his thieving from them; that either Kali Callender or one or more of the Redferns had killed him for impregnating young Madonna; or that he had cheated another, as yet unknown drug dealer, and had been on the receiving end of the usual reprisal, though in this latter case, Casey was surprised that he hadn't been shot or knifed rather than bludgeoned to death.

Three of the commune members, Foxy and Jethro Redfern and Dylan Harper, had shown themselves to have hasty tempers. Kali Callender struck him as the devious sort who would seize her opportunity quietly and efficiently and most likely get away with it.

As for Scott 'Mackenzie' Johnson and Randy Matthews, Moon had implied they were both too wet to bludgeon someone to death. Though that didn't mean they wouldn't do it if sufficiently provoked. Maybe Callender had continually taunted them about their homosexuality. In spite of his 'right on' membership of a hippie commune, Callender, as the nastiest sort of red-blooded heterosexual male, struck Casey as the type to goad pitilessly. Had he goaded the pair once too often? Scott Johnson had seemed very protective of his much younger lover: had he struck out in his defence?

Casey sighed, because while he could ponder all he wished he was still powerless to effect an arrest or even to check much out except at a discreet distance. It frustrated him unendurably, a frustration increased all the more by Moon and Star's hopeless attempts to recall the movements of the rest during the critical hours before DaisyMay's body was found.

Because of all this, the case looked like proving a long haul.

But, as Casey heard the front door bang, heralding Rachel's return from her shopping trip, he knew he had to put the case aside for now. With the long hours he worked he had always striven to keep his promises to her. And this afternoon he had promised her a trip to one of the local stately homes. He had also promised her a picnic if the weather was fine and one look out of the window told him the day was set fair.

For now, he abandoned his notes and set to putting the food together. It didn't take long; it was a simple meal of chicken, salad and French bread. He had made the salad earlier and he had cooked the chicken the previous night.

Maybe time away from thinking about the commune murders would help him come to the truth.

Rachel must have glanced into the living room on her way through to the kitchen because she said, 'Not been working on the deaths at the commune all morning?'

'Just jotting things down while my mind was fresh,' Casey defended himself. 'Everything's ready for our day out.' He picked up the picnic basket from the kitchen counter and held it aloft as proof.

'Let me have a piece of that bread,' she said. 'I'm starved.'

'Too busy spending to have a bite to eat?' he teased. To judge from the quantity of carrier bags, he wasn't far wrong.

'A girl has to replenish her wardrobe, Will. It's a feminine necessity.' She took the piece of bread that Casey had cut for her, spread a generous helping of butter and took a large bite. She said nothing more till the bread was but a memory. 'Mmm, I was ready for that. Are we all set?'

'All set.'

'Good. I'll just go to the bathroom and we'll be off. And,' she reminded him in case he had forgotten her earlier instructions, 'this afternoon is "us" time. No wandering off to thoughts of murder.'

'I hear and I will obey, oh mistress.' Since he had already promised he was hers for the afternoon, he would have no compunction about relegating his parents and their problems to the back of his mind. Maybe it would even be the best place for them. It might, as he had earlier thought, throw up some possibilities which his conscious mind hadn't thought of. He opened the front door as Rachel descended the stairs and he slammed it firmly behind them and on any further anxious thoughts about the commune. Soon enough, the worry thereof.

Six

On the following Monday, Casey and Rachel's short break came to an end. It was as Casey was getting ready for work that Catt rang him to report there had been a vicious killing on their home patch, so now, along with their unofficial investigation, they had the long hours of an *official* one to contend with. Casey had no idea how they were to cope with both.

And as he hurriedly dried after his shower and threw his clothes on, Casey suspected that things were about to get a whole lot more difficult. His return to work would naturally severely curtail whatever time they had to continue with the shadowy investigation of the two commune deaths. And ThomCatt had been carrying out his part of the inquiries after duty hours, which would be few enough now with this latest murder.

Casey found a moment to regret the loss of leisure hours. Such precious time had enabled him to think. But now the demands of work would impinge. Not that he'd been thinking with razor sharpness anyway since Moon had broken the news of the commune deaths, though that was more down to lack of solid information than lack of effort. And given his limited ability to contact his mother, as well as his lack of contacts in the Boston area, he was heavily dependent on his streetwise and frequently maverick sergeant. But, to be fair, so far, ThomCatt had done a sterling ferreting job; much better, certainly, than he had been in a position to do.

That was the frustration, of course. Casey desperately needed to be able to do *something*. Anything. But as he drove to the murder scene through the narrow streets of the medieval centre of town that was the bane of modern-day motorists, past the timber framing and over-hanging first floor jetties that shaded out most of the light, Casey warned himself against such unwise desires. Following their natural instincts was what had landed his parents in their current unfortunate predicament, never mind a number of preceding ones. Was he now, after so many years of trying to avoid following in his parents' foolhardy and irresponsible footsteps, to start to backtrack in his determinedly opposing path? Such a move would be foolhardy indeed.

The King's Langley murder victim had been found half an hour before Casey returned to work. It looked set to become an unpleasant case. Not only did the victim have the knife wound to his groin, but his penis had been cut off and stuffed in his mouth as a last hurrah.

And when, shortly after, Casey stood at the scene, biting wind and rain painfully slapping his trousers against his chilled legs, he had to force himself to treat any weakening emotion as dispassionately as the wind treated his legs. But, as a man, the manner of this victim's death cut to his soul, not to mention cutting his masculinity to shreds.

The victim, who looked to be around his late thirties, had certainly died an unpleasant, lonely death if the wounds to his body and the body's location were indicative. Dr Merriman, the pathologist, when he had finally arrived from his home twenty miles distant, told Casey in his thin, unemotional voice, that the knife had severed the femoral artery, causing the victim to lose a large quantity of blood

'Doesn't look like he was killed here,' he added as he knelt beside the half-naked victim. 'And though you'll have to wait for the post-mortem to get confirmation, I think I can safely say he bled to death.'

Casey nodded. But, like Dr Merriman, he wouldn't jump to hasty conclusions. The victim had probably bled to death, possibly in the alley where he had been found, though both the thoughts of Dr Merriman and the shortage of blood would seem to indicate this was not the case – but as the doctor had remarked, the post-mortem would confirm whether or not the body had been moved after death.

Casey found himself wishing the victim had been found in a more pleasant location than an alley. Surrounded by the fly-blown litter of takeaway cartons and used condoms, this seemed altogether too squalid and depressing a place for anyone to die. Even though he often, morbidly, contemplated his own death, Casey had never considered a death like this one.

'A gangland killing, you reckon, boss?' Catt asked as he came up behind him.

Casey heard Merriman tutting to himself at this supposition, but he ignored him and turned to answer Catt. He noticed his sergeant's hair, his pride and joy, had been liberally plastered with hairspray this morning to keep it in place whatever the weather might do to dislodge the perfectly coiffed locks. It looked as stiff as a board and about as movable. 'The viciousness certainly makes that a strong possibility, ThomCatt.' Casey had checked, but no identification had been found on the corpse. Either he hadn't carried anything or his killer had removed the victim's wallet in an attempt to delay identification. For now, at the start of the case, anything was possible.

For several more moments, Casey studied the body. The dead man was lying amongst the alley's detritus, curled into a foetal position. It was as if the body had accepted that death, and as many of the indignities it could contrive, would come for him on swift-winged heels and had tried to prepare for its arrival by protecting his remaining in situ private parts.

Casey took Catt's arm and drew him aside. They walked to the end of the alleyway, away from the busyness of the immediate scene and its milling forensic and photography teams. Away, too, from the shelter the alley provided. Catt pulled a face as the keening wind, stronger now away from the protection afforded by the alley's fencing, tried again and with a little more effect, to disturb his hairstyle. Even though Casey was anxious to have a word with Catt in private, he was too wary of the listening ears of the hovering cordoned-off neighbours and the even more acute ears of the stringers who fed stories to the national press to stray beyond the police cordon.

'Who found him?' Casey asked quietly.

'Some old bloke out walking his dog,' Catt told him. 'Name of Cedric Abernethy. Eighty if he's a day. He only lives along the way.' Catt nodded towards the line of terraced houses that backed on to the alley. 'Number fifty-two. He found the body at seven thirty. He said he always goes the back way, via the alley, when he takes his dog for his daily walks and the body wasn't there when he set off just before six.' In an undertone, Catt confided, 'And although this Mr Abernethy is a World War Two veteran, and made in the stiff-upper-lip tradition, I'd go easy on him. He was so shaken up by his discovery that the uniforms first on the scene let him return home. One of them is with him now.'

Casey nodded. 'Quite right. We don't want another death on our hands, particularly not that of a veteran.' Not in addition to the John Doe in the alley and the two unofficial bodies they already had. He paused. 'Do we know if this Mr Abernethy touched the body at all?'

'According to what he told uniform, he just checked the pulse in the victim's neck, but otherwise didn't disturb the body. He immediately got on the phone and rang nine-nine-nine.'

Casey nodded. 'We'd better speak to him now. Is he fit to be questioned?'

'I think so. But if you hang on a tick, I'll send one of the girlies along to check on him.'

Casey's green eyes showed his disapproval at this non-politically correct wording.

ThomCatt held up his hands in admission of guilt and said, 'Sorry, boss.' But the tiny grin which hovered at the corners of his mouth made a mockery of his own apology and of the PC brigade and all its works. Catt's insincere apology was further belied by his calling, 'Hey Annie, my darling, do me a favour?'

His non-PC approach did not seem to Casey to have caused the young female constable offence. On the contrary, she hurried towards Catt as if eager for more of his 'darlings'. But that was Tom: whatever he had that the female of the species liked, he had it in spades as the never-ending procession of girlfriends through Catt's bachelor flat proved. It was a talent that didn't win over Superintendent Brown-Smith, who was PC through and through and who heartily disapproved of Catt's easy ways.

The young woman officer was soon back with the information that Mr Abernethy was fit to be questioned.

Catt led the way around the corner to the front of the row of terraces, nodded to one of the uniformed officers outside Mr Abernethy's home and walked up the short path. Casey followed him.

Another uniform answered their knock and showed them into the small front sitting room with its solid, dark furniture which made the room seem even smaller than it was. Thickly patterned nets screened the windows and half their surface was covered by heavy drapes which made the room even darker. The room was like a cocoon against the modern world and Casey wondered, since he had found the bloodied remains of their John Doe, how safe Cedric Abernethy felt now behind its protective shell.

Mr Abernethy sat, looking quietly composed, in a well-worn, straight-backed armchair to the right of the meagre fire. Although certainly elderly and looking thin and frail, he sat with a military bearing and was clearly made of sterner stuff than he appeared.

But then, Casey reminded himself, their witness was of that generation who knew about hardship, be it on the battlefield or elsewhere. After quietly eliciting a few more brief facts, Casey, having been invited to sit in the matching and equally well-worn armchair on the opposite side of the fire, said, 'You told the uniformed officers that the man was dead when you found him, Mr Abernethy. Is that correct?'

Cedric Abernethy nodded. 'I've seen enough dead bodies in my time to recognize when the spirit has left.' The old man raised thick-veined and age-spotted hands from his knees before he let them fall again. 'No one could lose as much blood as that man must have – to judge by the stains on his trousers – and still survive. He was dead all right and had been for some time, I think.'

'Did you see anyone else around when you found the

body?' The man's assailant, having sliced open a main artery, was likely to be heavily bloodstained.

But, Casey soon learned, they weren't destined to have an early suspect in the investigation, because Mr Abernethy shook his head and told them, 'I saw no one. Not a soul, from the time me and Timothy left home to the time I returned and rang nine-nine-nine.' He stroked the rough, greying head of his terrier. The old dog gave a gruff 'woof', though whether this was to offer doggy comfort to his master or to confirm his words, Casey couldn't tell.

'I wondered, Mr Abernethy,' Casey said tentatively, 'whether the location of this man's death might indicate he was local. Did you recognize him?'

Again, Cedric Abernethy shook his head. 'I don't believe so. But I know few young people; they have little time for an old dodderer like me. Besides, so many young men look alike, don't they? With their heads half-scalped by the barber and with that scruffy stubbly growth of beard that simply looks slovenly. Grow a beard or don't grow a beard. That in-between look just appears messy and indicates a sloppy lack of personal hygiene. Shame they've done away with National Service. Some of today's young men could do with a sharp burst of military discipline.'

Mr Abernethy met Casey's gaze and gave a brief smile. 'Sorry. It's one of my hobby horses. But the appearance of young men these days is, I suppose, the same rule that says all old men look the same – bald, jowly and with glasses. The same rule seems to convince all old women that they have to perm their hair. Some sort of generational unofficial uniform.'

Mr Abernethy – neither bald, nor jowly, and with piercing grey eyes that wouldn't have shamed a bird of prey – clearly hadn't either voluntarily or involuntarily adopted the uniform of the aged male.

But, for all his composure, he was able to tell them nothing more. After thanking him for his help, Casey, feeling the question might be construed as an insult by the old soldier, asked if he was OK after the shock of finding the body or whether he would like him to contact his doctor.

'Thank you, no. I'm fine. Anyway, all he'll do is give me a sedative, thereby postponing any nightmares from tonight to tomorrow. What's the point of that? Not that I'm likely to suffer nightmares, anyway. I'm long past them now. Don't trouble yourself, Chief Inspector. I'll be all right. I've seen a lot worse in my time. But thank you for your concern.'

After he had handed Mr Abernethy a card and had extracted a promise that their witness would contact him if he recalled anything more, Casey left, with Catt at his heels.

'There's CCTV in the High Street and Carey Street,' Casey commented as they returned to the scene. 'Worth checking to see if our victim shows up.'

Catt nodded. 'I'll get straight on to it.'

By now, forensic and uniform between them and doubtless having struggled against the wind, had erected protective screening around the body. Having pronounced life extinguished and given his preliminary findings, Dr Merriman was on the verge of departure. He nodded a brisk goodbye to Casey and set off to the mortuary without another word.

Since they had left the scene to speak to Cedric Abernethy the number of gawping bystanders had grown. But as Casey had instructed, they and the press were herded to the far ends of the street in which the alleyway was found. Further guards were set at both ends of the alley in case some enterprising journalist attempted to gain an advantage over his colleagues. Such a precaution was a bit late, though, Casey noted. Already, one or two of the more forceful of the fourth estate were stationed at bedroom windows in the houses facing the alley. They must have bribed the householders to gain such a grandstand view. Casey, expecting shortly to feature in their rags himself over the commune killings, bit back an impotent sigh.

After watching forensic go about their painstaking routines for a few minutes, Casey said to ThomCatt, 'We can do nothing further here. I'll see you back at the station. Finding our victim's identity is our first priority.'

They fought their way through the crowds to their respective cars and drove to the station.

*　　*　　*

It didn't take long to retrieve the CCTV tapes and get the house-to-house questioning set in motion. But after viewing the tapes, Catt told Casey that the victim didn't feature on any of them.

'Must have been brought the back way and avoided the cameras,' he said.

Casey nodded. 'We'll just have to hope the house-to-house teams discover something, though as it seems he was dumped in that alleyway before most people stir out of their houses, the possibility of getting information from such a source is slim at best.'

Casey hated John Doe cases. At least with an immediate identity they had something to start from. But here, he would just have to hope the pictures of the dead man he had instructed the photographer to forward to the media brought forth some results.

As it happened, and though he had yet to discover this, finding out the victim's identity turned out to be the easy part. Unfortunately, discovering who had wanted the man dead and in such a way, looked likely to be a far more lengthy job.

Seven

Catt perched on the corner of the desk. He must have paid a visit to the gents' toilet since returning to the station, because his hair was now so immaculate one would never have thought the wind had dared to play with it. He swung his right leg as he awaited the allotment of another job. 'By the way,' he said to Casey, 'there's a woman in reception I think might interest you.'

'Oh yes?'

'I overheard her reporting her husband missing as I came back from viewing the CCTV footage and I hung around to earwig. Said husband sounds an awful lot like the John Doe we found in the alley. Even down to the clothes he was wearing.'

Casey snatched up the telephone and got through to the front office. 'You've a woman in reception who's reported her husband missing. Don't let her leave. I'm coming right down.' He asked the woman's name, replaced the receiver and hurried to the ground floor.

Casey entered reception and saw a tall, well-built woman at the counter. He walked towards her. 'Mrs Oliver?' he asked.

She nodded.

'I'm DCI Casey. I understand you've just reported your husband missing?'

'That's right.'

'Perhaps you'd like to come up to my office and we can talk?'

For a moment, Mrs Oliver looked vaguely alarmed at this invitation as if she would have felt easier talking to some junior officer. She certainly seemed surprised that an officer of his rank should concern himself with her missing husband. Then she gave a faint shrug and followed Casey to the locked door that led to the main body of the station. She waited while he keyed in the entry code. He opened the door and held it for her to go through.

Once in his office, he asked if she had a recent photo of her missing husband.

'Yes. I thought it would be useful, so I brought this.' She reached into her capacious handbag and, from one of the side pockets, pulled out a glossy eight by ten inch photo and handed it to him. 'That picture was taken last year. It's a good likeness.'

Casey nodded as he stared at the photo. There was no doubt that it was their John Doe. He stared for a few moments more at the photo as he gathered his thoughts and decided how to best break the news of her husband's violent death. But before he did that, he checked on what her husband had been wearing. As he'd expected, the clothing was a match for their cadaver.

'I'm afraid, Mrs Oliver, that from the evidence of the photograph and clothing, I have some bad news for you. A man answering your husband's description was found dead in an alley in the town this morning.'

She stared at him without uttering a sound, but her shock showed in the tightly-clenched fingers on the handles of her bag.

'Of course, to be certain, we need someone to identity the body. Is there someone, a relative, say, who could do that?'

Mrs Oliver shook her head.

'What about friends who know your husband well?'

She shook her head again and said, 'There's his work colleagues, of course, but I'd rather not trouble them. Besides, if the man you found is Gus, then I'm his widow.' She sat up straighter in Casey's visitor's chair and said with a determined edge to her voice, 'I'd prefer to do any identifying that's necessary.'

'Very well. If you're sure.' Defeated in his desire to spare her the ordeal of identifying the man who seemed likely to

be her husband, Casey tried another friendly overture. 'Have
you a neighbour who could stay with you?'

'No. There is no one.' She hesitated, then said, 'I need
to know, Chief Inspector. One way or the other. I need to
see him and know for certain.' Her voice became stilted as
she added, 'If I don't see the body I'll always wonder if it
was really my husband.' Her voice petered out and she sat
still and silent.

Casey broke into her reverie. 'Of course. Don't worry.
We'll take you along to view the body shortly, seeing as
there is no one else to do it. I'll get it organized. But
before I do that, I need confirmation of your husband's
name. You called him Gus. I presume that's short for
Augustus?'

'No. It's short for Gustav.'

'I see. Your husband was foreign, perhaps?' He hoped
not or it would widen the extent of the investigation consid-
erably.

'No. He is as English as you or me. The name was just
a fancy of his mother's.'

Relieved, Casey nodded and said, 'If you'll wait here,
I'll get that viewing arranged. I won't be long.' Casey left
his office and made for the main CID office; he didn't want
to talk about her dead husband in her presence. Perhaps he
was being unduly sensitive, but he thought a degree of sensi-
tivity was called for in the circumstances, especially as she
seemed to have no one to turn to, no friends or family to
support her.

Catt was hovering outside the door and he waylaid Casey
as he came out. 'So, what's the verdict?' he asked. 'Is our
cadaver this woman's missing husband?'

Casey nodded. 'Seems so. Mrs Oliver brought a photo
in and it's the dead spit of our John Doe. Our guy's name
is Gustav Oliver. Gus for short.'

Catt raised his eyes on hearing the dead man's first name
and through pursed lips he asked, 'Foreign, was he?'

'Not according to his widow. His mother just had
outlandish taste in names.'

'Good to get a confirmed ID so quickly, anyway.'

Casey nodded again and headed for the nearest CID desk to ring the mortuary.

The visit to the mortuary was soon organized and they were shortly on their way. As well as Catt, Casey had collected Shazia Khan, one of the station's female officers, to accompany them and provide support for Mrs Oliver during her identification ordeal. Dr Merriman had rung to tell them the post-mortem was scheduled for that afternoon. For Mrs Oliver's sake, Casey was thankful she would view the corpse before the post-mortem. Even though such viewings were arranged with as much delicacy as possible, the PM would naturally leave its mark and many found the ravages left behind on the body upsetting.

The journey to St Luke's, the local hospital, didn't take long. Neither did Mrs Oliver's examination of the body. After staring intently for several long moments, she confirmed the dead man's identity. She pulled a handkerchief from her coat pocket and dabbed at her eyes before turning away for some much needed privacy. After giving her several minutes in which to compose herself, Casey took her arm and ushered her gently out of the viewing room. 'I'll take you home,' he told her.

Once back in the car, he said, 'I'll need to ask you some questions about Mr Oliver's movements, but that can wait till tomorrow if you prefer.' For himself, he would like to find out as much as possible as soon as possible, but Oliver's widow was entitled to some consideration. Even so, he was relieved when she declined his offer.

'I'd rather get any questioning over and done with, Chief Inspector,' she replied. 'Get all the unpleasantness over in one go.'

'As you wish. But we can take you home and interview you there.'

As Alice Oliver gave directions to her home, Casey realized how shockingly close her house was to the alley where her dead husband was discovered by Cedric Abernethy; she might have stumbled over his corpse herself. She would now have to pass the alley every day as, although in different streets, her home and the alley where her husband's body was found were separated by little more than fifty yards, the alley being in a quiet road which led to the centre of town.

Mrs Oliver's home was an imposing detached house with a double garage situated in a short cul-de-sac. It was a modern house but featured several Georgian adornments, like a pedestal over the front door and a uniform alloca-tion of expensive modern sash windows. The house was in a mixed neighbourhood with large, detached properties mingling cheek by jowl with cramped Victorian terraced houses similar to the one around the corner in which Cedric Abernethy lived.

According to Alice Oliver, once they had arrived at her comfortable but plainly furnished home and were seated in her double-aspect drawing room, her husband had left the house around nine o'clock on Friday evening. It was now Monday.

Puzzled, Casey asked, 'Why didn't you report him missing earlier, Mrs Oliver? You must have been worried.'

'Yes. Of course I was, but I didn't think you would take my worries seriously when he'd been missing such a short time. Only children merit such immediate concern. Gus is – was – an adult, after all. It was only when another night came and went and he still hadn't returned that I felt justi-fied in reporting him missing. He often stayed away from home overnight, you see. Sometimes for two nights, without telephoning me, so I wasn't unduly worried. But, of course, when two nights stretched into three, I knew something must be badly wrong.'

'I see.'

Now that they had a confirmed ID, Casey said gently, 'There are one or two matters we need to put to you.'

She frowned. 'What matters? I've already told you what time he left home. What else can you possibly want to know? Unless I was mistaken about his identity?' She broke off and stared at Casey. 'Tell me,' she said, 'tell me, please. Could I have been mistaken or is the man found dead in that alley really my husband?'

Casey was quick to dispel any rising hope. 'I'm afraid the similarities are too apparent for there to be any doubt. I'm sorry.'

She nodded and gave him a brief, wavering smile. 'I just hoped—' She broke off. 'Never mind. I suppose everyone in my position indulges in some wishful thinking. But I see I must face facts.' She got up and made for the door. 'I'll put the kettle on. I'm sure you'd like tea.'

Once she had left the room he turned as Catt touched his arm. Catt whispered that he had rung the station from the mortuary to alert the murder team that they had a definite confirmed ID. During the call he had learned that several other women had rung in after they had seen the dead man's photograph on the news bulletin – the media hadn't rested on their laurels, but then neither had Casey. He had asked the police photographer to forward the man's photo plus the bare details, which was all they had themselves, to one of his contacts amongst the local television news team. The item had featured in the final slot that morning. It had certainly hit the target, because these women, too, had given the dead man's name as Gus Oliver.

Mrs Oliver came back with the tea. She had even troubled to fill a plate with biscuits. It was a thoughtful gesture in the midst of her grief and Casey was touched.

It was clear she had been thinking whilst in the kitchen, because as she placed the tray with the tea things on a small side table, poured the tea and passed the cups, she said, 'If my husband is dead, murdered, surely, isn't it more important for you to set about finding who killed him than questioning me?'

'Yes, of course,' Casey answered. 'But your answers to my questions will hopefully help us to find his killer. They are important. For instance, we need to know of anyone who might have had reason to harm your husband. Do you know if he had any enemies?'

'Enemies? No. Everyone loved Gus. He was a very popular man.'

Casey was careful to avoid meeting Thomas Catt's eye, as he helped himself to milk, certain he would see the message 'popular with the ladies, anyway' writ large there. According to the information Catt had whispered, the late Mr Oliver wasn't of a retiring nature where the ladies were concerned. Of course that might mean they had just been friends or business acquaintances of Oliver's. Casey would not let himself be influenced by Catt's knowing wink. As yet, he had no way of knowing if Gus Oliver's widow had been aware of her husband's extra-marital activities – if such they were – and now was not the time to question her on the matter. Certainly she was unaware of the number of women in his life who, like her, had already contacted them and identified him. But given the apparent number of them, he found it improbable that she could have remained in ignorance. He frowned as he realized that Catt's knowing wink and manner were already influencing him towards the extra-marital romances scenario. She must at least have suspected what her husband was up to. Determinedly, he added to himself – *If* he was up to anything.

Still, for now, he would give her the benefit of the doubt. They were likely to find plenty of indications from other witnesses as to whether Mrs Oliver had known of her husband's women friends.

Mrs Oliver hesitated, sipped her tea as if she hoped to gain strength from the hot liquid, then added, 'Though, I suppose, as he was such a successful businessman he must have attracted some ill-wishers. After all, someone hated him enough to murder him.'

'Do you know where he went on these all-night trips?' Casey questioned.

'Rarely. Gus didn't confide in me about business matters. Why do you ask? Do you suspect that he might have been killed by a business rival?'

'It's one possibility.' Casey paused, then, thinking of the viciousness of the murder that, as Catt had remarked, held the hallmarks of a gangland slaying, asked as delicately as he could, 'Did he have any dealings with shady types? People on the fringes of crime, perhaps? So many of the more clever criminals nowadays have bona fide businesses alongside their illegal ones, so it's possible he might have, unknowingly, done business with one or two.'

'I've no idea. As I said, my husband didn't confide his business dealings to me.'

That was a pity, was Casey's immediate thought. It meant they would have to do some serious digging into these presumed violent business rivals.

'You might contact his secretary,' Alice Oliver said. 'She should be able to give you more information. She's a nice young woman, by the name of Caroline Everett. I believe she's worked for Gus for several years. '

Casey nodded as Catt noted the name, then asked, 'Did your husband have a home office? Somewhere where we might find an address book of friends and business contacts?'

'Yes. It's in the spare bedroom. I'll show you.' She put her cup down and led them up the stairs to her husband's office.

'We'd also like to see your husband's bedroom, Mrs Oliver,' Casey said.

'If you must. It's the door at the top of the stairs.'

'We'll look at the office first. Have we your permission to take away with us anything we think might be relevant to your husband's death?'

'Take what you like and welcome,' she said. 'I have no use for any of it.'

Fortunately, Gus Oliver had been a tidy man; everything was neatly compartmentalized – much like his love life, thought Casey. They quickly found a business address book. A search through his filing cabinet and desk drawers revealed little of interest. He seemed to use both just for household bills and other domestic paperwork

Next, they investigated the bedroom. Catt eyed the single bed with a narrowed gaze. 'Looks like things weren't hunky-dory on the marital front.'

'Not necessarily. Lots of married people prefer to sleep separately. Perhaps Gus Oliver was a champion snorer?' Still, it was, as Catt had said, an interesting aspect of the Olivers' life together, though he refused to give a fillip to ThomCatt's salaciousness on the matter. But, taken together with the other women who had telephoned . . .

As in the office, they found little of interest in the bedroom. There were no incriminating slips of paper in the pockets of Oliver's jackets or trousers or anywhere else; either the dead man had memorized his women friends' addresses and telephone numbers or he kept such incriminating details at work. After obtaining the location of Gus Oliver's business premises, they asked Mrs Oliver if she would like Shazia Khan to stay with her. She refused the offer, telling them she preferred to be alone. 'After all, it's something I'm going to have to get used to.'

They bid her farewell as there was nothing else they could offer by way of comfort and made for the station.

'It's unfortunate that Gus Oliver gives every appearance of being a serial philanderer,' Catt commented as they drove away. 'Just think of the number of jealous women and angry husbands who could have wanted to off him. Not to mention a possibly jealous – with reason – wife.'

'Don't,' Casey pleaded. 'I'm trying not to think about the potential number of suspects. Don't forget, there's also the business angle. Mr Oliver, to judge from his home, was a wealthy and successful man. It's possible he didn't always use nice methods to bring in the cash.'

'Judging from the ugliness of his death, it looks like he wasn't the only one with less than nice ways to him.'

Once back at the station, Casey stopped off at the incident room. Several more women had rung up to identify the dead man during the time they had been out; foolishly, although failing to give their names or other details, in their distress, they had rung from their home telephone numbers and were thus easily traced. He handed the details to Catt. 'Go and see them and the others who have rung in. Find out if any of them have alibis for the relevant times. Check if they hold water. Take Shazia Khan with you. Meanwhile, I'll go to Oliver's business premises and see what I can find out.'

Catt nodded, took the list and left the office.

Casey shrugged back into his coat and set off for Oliver's work place.

*   *   *

The business premises of Oliver's International was on the edge of King's Langley, on the industrial estate that had been built five years ago just off the bypass. The building was three stories high. Sleek, black and glossy, it was starkly modern with lots of glass and with a car park for around thirty cars in front.

The glossy theme continued inside. The floor was black marble, as was the large reception desk. Casey thought it somewhat funereal, as all the black was only relieved by modern, abstract pictures which, from what he gleaned by a quick peer at the paintings, were by Jackson Pollock. Piles of the firm's literature were heaped on the small tables dotting the reception area. He helped himself to one of each before he crossed to the reception desk. After producing his ID and telling the elegant, much-painted young woman behind the desk that he needed to speak to Mr Oliver's secretary – thinking she would be the quickest route to finding out about Oliver's business affairs – he was instructed to sit down while she rang through to her office. He settled down to reading the firm's literature while he waited.

It seemed Oliver's International dealt in the import of decorative exotica from around the world; everything from African wooden masks to rugs and other textiles, as well as skilfully crafted metalwork from India and the Middle East. The business was aimed at the wealthy and successful and its goods seemed to be priced accordingly, as per a separate price list which Casey had picked up. Briefly, he wondered if their imports had included drugs: it would certainly explain the gangland appearance of Oliver's killing. But before he ventured down that road he wanted to find out a lot more about the victim and his lifestyle. Certainly, from what they had learned so far they had sufficient potential suspects to be going on with without seeking out Colombian drug barons.

The office of Caroline Everett, Oliver's secretary, was also large and glossy. It adjoined her boss's. She proved very helpful once she got over the shock of her boss's murder. She was an attractive girl, a strawberry blonde with a willowy figure, but given Oliver's propensity for numerous affairs, which propensity Casey was gradually coming to accept, he supposed it was a prerequisite that his female staff should be young and good-looking.

Once seated in her office, Casey asked Caroline Everett if Gus Oliver had had any rancorous disputes with one or more of his rival business acquaintances that might have led to his brutal death.

To Casey's surprise, she said, 'I'm afraid so.' Her accompanying smile was long-suffering and wry. 'I don't like to speak ill of the dead and he wasn't a bad boss to work for, but if you were a business rival who trod on his corns – look out.' She sat down behind her desk and invited Casey to take a chair.

'Mr Oliver could be ruthless. He liked to get his own way and often played dirty. He loved nothing better than a good row, the more acrimonious the better. He was always involved in some dispute or other. In fact, we're currently involved in several court cases.'

'Is that so?' Casey sat up and whipped out his notebook. 'I'd appreciate the details of the other parties and what the disputes were about.'

They didn't take long to produce. Casey returned his notebook to his pocket as Caroline quickly typed the details and the nature of the various disputes and printed them out. Attractive *and* efficient, was Casey's thought. Not a common mix. Beautiful people were seldom expected to be other than decorative in his experience. But he supposed Gus Oliver had been the sort of man to demand the best in all things. Competence, like beauty, was undoubtedly another prerequisite.

'You said Mr Oliver wasn't a bad boss to work for,' Casey remarked.

'That's right. Most of the time, anyway. It was only when he got deeply involved in some rancorous dispute that he could become snappy. But, on the whole, once he'd got over the fact that I had no intention of joining his harem, he wasn't a bad boss to work for.'

'So you knew about his infidelities?'

'Hard not to as I was the one deputed to buying Valentine's cards and birthday flowers and jewellery.'

'What about his wife? Did you know her well?'

Caroline shook her head. 'Hardly at all. She rarely came to the office and telephoned almost as seldom. As far as I could tell they mostly seemed to lead separate lives.'

'Did she know about her husband's affairs?'

'I've no idea. But she must have done, surely? As I said, I can't know for sure, but it seems likely given the amount of time he must have spent away from home evenings and weekends. But Mrs Oliver is not a gossipy woman. She's always been perfectly civil to me but we never got on first name terms. Not that she rang very often. I've always thought her quite a formal, reserved type. Maybe the neighbours will know more?'

Casey doubted it from what Alice Oliver had said. 'Perhaps you could supply me with a list of your boss's lady friends?' It would be interesting to see if the list Caroline supplied matched the list they had already compiled from the phone calls made by Oliver's many female acquaintances.

List in hand, he thanked Caroline Everett for her help and made for the car park. Later, they would have to go through Oliver's office files and see if they discovered more likely killers amongst the paperwork. But, for the meantime, they had enough, between his love trysts and his business disputes, to keep them busy.

Eight

As Casey, assisted by the wind which was still blowing with gusto, walked back to the car to return to the station he acknowledged that he and Catt would need to speak to Mrs Oliver again and find out what – if anything – she knew about her husband's extramarital affairs.

But first, they would concentrate on the ladies who had so carelessly telephoned without taking the precaution of using a public phone or of dialling 141 on their home phones to conceal their identity. He'd let Catt finish checking them out before he spoke to Mrs Oliver again and see if they could provide alibis. It would be interesting to get Catt's take on the women. Any who failed to provide a verifiable alibi he would go to see himself.

On the drive back to the station, he mused about the case. On the face of it, by ringing the incident room to tell them of the dead man's identity, these women friends of Oliver's had given themselves the aura of innocence. 'I rang you as soon as I recognized him,' they would say, 'but as for knowing anything about his death . . .'

But it was an innocence Casey put no trust in. Because innocent or guilty, each of the women must secretly believe that their liaisons with Oliver would come out. If one of the women had murdered him, by phoning in they were covering their tracks and making themselves appear virtuous by helping the police in their investigation. More suspicious for them *not* to telephone, they would surely have thought, when Gus Oliver's photo had received such wide publicity in the local media.

Once back at the station and before he left again to attend the post-mortem, Casey rang the three business rivals with whom Oliver had been in dispute to make appointments. He wondered how Catt was getting on in questioning Oliver's harem. More ladies had since rung in, so he hoped Catt would be able to quickly eliminate one or two of those from the first list. But he didn't worry about it unduly. He'd find out the results of Catt's interviews soon enough. Meanwhile, he had interviews of his own to arrange. He'd told Catt he'd see him at the mortuary. He would speak to his sergeant after the post-mortem and find out what he had discovered.

Dr Merriman adjusted the microphone under his chin and began the post-mortem. Not by nature a garrulous or sociable man, he didn't pause to provide asides to Casey and Catt; rather, once he'd identified the cadaver on the slab and given his measurements, he directed all his words to the mike.

'Deep knife wound to the left groin area. Femoral artery severed, which is the probable cause of death. A kitchen carving knife could have done it. He would have bled to death fairly rapidly. The removal of the victim's penis looks to have occurred after death, but I'll confirm that one after toxicological analysis. The hypostasis evidence shows the victim was moved after death and didn't die in the alleyway where his body was found.' Dr Merriman's thin, dry voice droned remorselessly on. As usual, he had been noncommittal at the murder scene, but now, with the post-mortem underway, he confirmed his previous suspicions with that irritating, lecturing tone that had always grated on Casey. But he didn't let his feelings show any more than Merriman. He simply watched, impassively, as Merriman made his first, long incision, from chest to groin.

Unusually for him, Casey had begun to drift off. He now had a definite cause of death as well as the identity of the victim. Dr Merriman had already confirmed his findings that the victim had been dead for between forty-eight and sixty hours when he had been found. Now all he lacked was the location of the murder and its perpetrator. Although he had little liking for the pathologist, Casey was grateful to him for confirming the body had been moved after death. It might just reduce the number of suspects who could have relocated it. And even if it didn't do that, any car used in its transportation would surely not escape without some bloodstains.

The post-mortem eventually drew to a close. Casey and Catt left immediately, Merriman being no more inclined to chat after the procedure than he was during it. Anyway, they had their answers.

There had been no chance to talk during the post-mortem, Dr Merriman disliking what he called idle chatter while he worked, but once they got into the fresh air and away from the abattoir stench, Casey asked Catt how he'd got on during his interviews with Oliver's lovers who featured on their earliest list.

'All three are doing shocked, stunned and saddened to perfection,' Catt began brightly. 'Though funnily enough, if one or more of them are merely friends, they're all very attractive, which I thought a bit of a coincidence. But we don't have to rely on supposition as it was clear from the wary manner of all three that their friendships with Oliver were rather more than platonic. Amanda Meredith, Sarah Garrett and Carole Brown all claim to have been at home between nine and midnight on Friday night,' Catt told him.

'Any witnesses?'

'Amanda Meredith claims her husband was at home, too, working in his home office at the top of the house.'

'Easy enough for her to slip out then. Mrs Garrett and Ms Brown were both home alone?'

Catt confirmed it.

'That's a shame. It would have been good to remove some of these women from the suspect list early on.'

'Mmm. By the way, I thought it might interest you to know that Carole Brown's partner is Max Fallon. You know, the bloke who owns King's nightclub in the town along with several more round and about. He features on the computer as having a tendency to violence, though he's only been charged with the odd petty offence. And, apart from these other women, let's not forget Mrs Oliver herself.

She had even more reason to be jealous than the members of Oliver's harem and their partners. And she's got one hell of a motive. We know she was home alone, too.'

'True. But he'd been unfaithful many times over it seems. Probably for a number of years, too. Why would she suddenly decide to do something about it, particularly something as violent as Oliver's murder?'

'Perhaps the quantity of extramarital activities became too much to bear and she wanted revenge.'

Casey shook his head. 'No. it doesn't feel right. Besides, taking him for a large chunk of his fortune in a divorce sounds like a far better revenge to me: each time you spent some of it you could enjoy the revenge all over again. And I think, in her case, there would need to be something else other than his women friends to persuade her to murder. Anyway, Tom, good work.' Casey handed Catt the latest additions to the list of Oliver's lovers. 'You've done so well I'd like you to check these ladies out also.'

'No hardship if they're anything like the first lot of lovelies.' Catt took the list and put it in his pocket.

'And I'll need to speak to all three of Oliver's so far un-alibied harem, of course. Set up appointments for me, please.'

Catt nodded. 'What about their husbands or partners? They would have a strong motive for wanting Oliver dead. The partners of the women with alibis will also need to be checked out. I wasn't able to speak to any of them as they were all at work. But if I make the first appointments for mid-evening this week, hopefully most of them will be home.'

Casey nodded. 'Do that.'

Casey rang Moon again that evening. He was alone in his office; Catt had still not returned from interviewing the latest batch of Oliver's lovers.

'Anything happened?' he asked Moon once they'd exchanged the usual greetings.

'Not a lot,' Moon replied. 'Apart from the fact that one of the kids has been sent home from school with suspected mumps.'

Casey swallowed his irritation with this inconsequential information as Moon went on. 'We're waiting for the doctor to call.' In spite of her current predicament, Moon managed a laugh. 'You should see the carry on of the men here,' she told Casey. 'They insisted Billy was confined to his room. Terrified, they are – apart from our widower, Dylan Harper.'

'Understandable, I suppose,' Casey replied, realizing he would have to humour her if she was to supply anything useful. Moon was not a woman to be rushed. 'Mumps can have an unfortunate effect on a grown man's fertility. And as for the widower, I would think he's got enough other things to be worried about at the moment.' He edged the conversation around to the area he *did* want to discuss. 'Are the local police still there?'

'Only a solitary constable. And the forensics people are still working on the apple orchard where DaisyMay was found, but I expect they'll finish for the night shortly.' Moon gave another sly chuckle. 'I think maybe the mumps frightened the rest off.'

'Have there been any more arguments in the house?' When he had last spoken to her, Moon had told him that everyone at the smallholding was blaming each other for the deaths.

'You could say that. There's been nothing but rows. So much for brotherly love, hey hon? The atmosphere is so lacking in the spiritual that if we were allowed to leave here me and Star would invite ourselves to your place for a bit of peace and love.'

Casey thanked God for the rigorous restrictions of a police investigation: his home had barely recovered from their last visit. It wasn't that he didn't love his parents; he just preferred them to remain at an unembarrassing distance from anyone he knew, particularly colleagues. He was aware that he had been lucky so far, in that only ThomCatt knew of the hippie parents. He wanted it to stay that way.

Telling Moon to stay calm, Casey bid her goodbye and rang off after reminding her that he would ring again the next evening.

At least she hadn't managed to misplace the mobile, which

was a minor miracle in itself. But they were still making little progress in the murders at the commune. Hardly surprising, given that ThomCatt was kept busy on the official enquiry. But Catt had at least managed to remove Callender's main drug dealer, Tony Magann, from the list of suspects. He still had feelers out with various of his contacts and Casey was hopeful that something might be shaken loose. Meanwhile, he awaited Catt's return from interviewing Gus Oliver's other girlfriends.

Gus Oliver really had turned out to be something of a local Lothario Catt confirmed on his return. And since a copy of the photo Alice Oliver had produced had been released, the number of ladies ringing the incident room claiming to be his girlfriend had crept into double figures.

'So, what have you got, Tom?' Casey enquired as he entered the office. 'Not too many more decent suspects, I hope?'

'Your hope is fulfilled, oh master. All of these latest women that I was able to see were able to provide alibis that were verified by more than one person.'

Casey was relieved to learn they were beginning to reduce numbers.

'I've got another few yet to see. I'll do that tomorrow.'

Someone had started a book on how many girlfriends would eventually claim the dead man as their lover. Catt had placed a bet before the likely numbers increased still further. Not having gained his 'ThomCatt' nickname for his sense of curiosity alone, he was moved to observe, 'Better make sure I never end up dead in an alley, boss, or you'll all be doing eighteen-hour days.'

Casey smiled. 'True. But, I suppose, given my knowledge of your habits, I might have the best chance of winning the pot.'

'You might if you actually gambled. No, to avoid you losing out, I'll just have to stay out of dark alleys.'

'Good of you.'

'I aim to please.'

*　　*　　*

By late afternoon the next day, Catt had interviewed the
rest of Gus Oliver's lovers and their partners. The latest
additions had all managed to provide alibis that had, so far,
checked out, as had their partners'. That left the original
three to be re-interviewed.

'Even with this latest batch of females seemingly out of
the running, we've no shortage of suspects,' ThomCatt
remarked laconically. 'We've still got three jealous husbands,
ditto girlfriends or women spurned, the betrayed wife, ruthless business rivals. Seems like we've got ourselves the full
clutch.'

Casey nodded. 'There's also the possibility that we're on
the wrong tack altogether. This killing could be a mugging
gone wrong and the cutting an attempt to suggest otherwise, especially with the victim's wallet missing.'

According to Mrs Oliver, whom Casey had telephoned,
the wealthy victim had been known to habitually carry large
sums of cash in his wallet – 'Probably didn't want to risk
his wife checking his bank and credit card statements for
fancy hotel interludes,' Catt commented before he added,
'though the mugging gone wrong scenario wouldn't surprise
me. Our Mr Oliver strikes me as having been one of life's
takers. I don't suppose he'd relish handing over his fat wallet
to some thug. Maybe he would have kept his life if he'd
been a giver rather than a taker.'

'Maybe so. Still, if that's what happened, it's odd that
the body was moved.' But Casey put that niggle aside for
the moment. He would think about it later. 'And now, as
we've uncovered Gus Oliver's many infidelities, before we
speak to the Merediths, Garretts or Carole Brown and her
partner, it's time we questioned his wife again. It will be
interesting to discover whether she admits to knowing about
some of these ladies. Let's get ourselves around there to
speak to her. Now that we know more about his love life,
Mrs Oliver might be more forthcoming. Find Shazia Khan
to take with us, will you, Tom?'

Casey was surprised, when they rang the Olivers' doorbell,
that Mrs Oliver herself opened the door. Even though she had
laid claim to no family, friends or helpful neighbours, Casey

was surprised she hadn't managed to rustle *someone* up. He decided he would leave Shazia Khan with her so she wasn't bothered by reporters. Casey, thinking again of the number of women who had rung in to say it *was* Gus Oliver's body which had been found in the alleyway, waited till they were seated once again in the large, plain drawing room before he attempted to ask any questions. He soon began to feel over-heated by the fires burning in the grates at either end of the room.

Mrs Oliver apologized for the furnace heat. 'I can't seem to get warm since my visit to the mortuary.'

Casey nodded understandingly. It was something that often affected him similarly: Catt seemed impervious to the chill factor of such places. 'We're quite all right,' he assured her. He paused, and was about to ask whether she had known about her husband's philandering, when she saved him the trouble.

After directing a sad smile at him, she said bluntly, 'As I imagine you've already discovered, Chief Inspector, since you issued his photograph to the media, my husband was a very popular man. Perhaps I should clarify that statement? He was popular with one gender. The female one. He had a lot of lady friends. I imagine that, by now, you must have heard from a number of them?'

Casey simply nodded and lowered his head in embar-rassed acknowledgement.

'There's no need to be uncomfortable, Chief Inspector. I've known about my husband's weakness for a long time. Not that I could be sure with which of his various lady friends he was disporting himself at any one time.'

'I see.' Casey glanced at Catt, who raised his eyebrows. Possible motive? the raised eyebrows asked in repetition of his earlier theory. Casey gave a slight shrug of the shoul-ders that said, Wait and see.

Now Alice Oliver changed tack and went off in a different direction. It was as if she dismissed her husband's women as no more than his shallow playthings and unlikely to feature on their suspect list. 'You asked before about possible business enemies. And although my husband never said anything, there must have been some. After all, when a man repeatedly cheats on his wife he's likely also to cheat others. That he had a whole host of enemies seems a likely possibility.' She frowned then and, as if she regretted her earlier easy dismissal of them, added, 'Including women he dumped or otherwise treated badly.'

'And do you know the names of any of these ladies?'

'I can give you some of them. But there are likely to be a few with whom I am unfamiliar.'

She reached across to the desk beside her armchair, pulled out a pad and pen and proceeded to jot down names and addresses.

There were half a dozen women on the list. Casey had to admire Gus Oliver's energy and his financial well-being; keeping so many women satisfied on the sexual and spending fronts must be costly in both. Several of the women already featured on their latest lists and had been exonerated.

'There's also his illegitimate daughter, of course. Caitlin Osborne. She was adopted and lived in Liverpool until about two weeks ago. When I rang Caitlin's adoptive parents so they could break the news of her father's death, I learned that Caitlin had left home around then. They have no idea where she might be. I'm afraid she had become rather fixated with Gus. When she was eighteen she managed to trace him. But he didn't want anything to do with her and refused to see her or answer any of her letters. She's something of a sad case. In and out of psychiatric hospitals since her early teens according to her adoptive parents. She's had a few psychotic episodes owing to her drug-taking.'

'Do you have Ms Osborne's address?' Casey asked.

She nodded and gave it. Catt noted it down. 'Though as I said, you won't find her there.'

'Tell me, Mrs Oliver,' Casey asked, 'how did you find out the identities of your husband's women friends?'

'I make – *made* – it my business to know who they are, Chief Inspector, and what kind of threat they pose –' again she quickly corrected herself – '*posed* to my marriage.' She found a smile; it was bittersweet with the pain of her knowledge. 'I had the advantage over his other women. I knew that Gus was commitment phobic. Once any of them became clingy and demanding, Gus dropped them. It was strange that he committed sufficiently to marry me. But then, I imagine he sensed that I would be the sort of wife who would put up with his extramarital activities. And having a wife already provides a fine excuse for a man like Gus to avoid deeper entanglements.' Her voice became even more pained as she admitted, 'I suppose you could say that I was perfect for him. As to how I found out about these women, I hired a private detective, Chief Inspector. I thought, as his wife, I was entitled to know what my husband was doing. Still, it was a shock to discover the extent of his infidelity. I've been planning to divorce him since I received the private detective's report. My husband, of course, had no idea I knew of his doings. He carried on with his infidelities in blissful ignorance that I was aware of them.'

'You said nothing to him?' Casey asked after obtaining the name of the private investigator. He was incredulous that any woman could keep such knowledge to herself. Perhaps his incredulity was evident in his voice because Alice Oliver shrugged and said, 'I saw no reason to give him time to provide himself with some spurious excuses before I instigated divorce proceedings. I wanted to get my own case ready first and make sure I knew as much about his investments as I could for the financial settlement in the divorce.'

It sounded remarkably cold-blooded to Casey. But perhaps, with the increasing years of marriage and similarly increasing infidelities, she had become as inured to her husband's behaviour as any woman could be and was, as he had suggested to Catt earlier, determined simply to make sure she was nicely set up for a comfortable future.

But the way her fingers knotted together in her lap indicated how hurt and diminished she really felt, as did her next words. 'I was never enough for him. I suppose I suspected it from the beginning. But I loved him, so up till now I've put up with his straying.' She gazed down at her hands, unknotted the fingers and looked up. 'I suppose you think me a foolish woman for cleaving to him through all his infidelities?' Her voice faltered as she added, 'And now I've lost him anyway.'

Casey tried to offer some words of comfort. 'We all, I suppose, do what we feel we need to do, in relationships as in life.' His thoughts briefly strayed to his own relationship with his parents. As with Alice Oliver and her husband, Casey knew he had never been enough for his parents. A fact of which he had been conscious for most of his life. But now was not the time to dwell on that. As the victim's widow, Mrs Oliver was entitled to his full attention.

But Mrs Oliver had little more to say. She had laid her pain bare for them. Casey thought that all three of them were relieved when they left shortly after, Mrs Oliver's list of her husband's paramours in Casey's pocket and Detective Constable Shazia Khan left behind to render Mrs Oliver some womanly comfort and to fend off the press.

Nine

The next morning Casey had a number of appointments strung out over the day. He had been able to fix up interviews with all four of Oliver's business rivals with whom he was in legal or other disputes. It would be interesting to meet the men involved in these slanging matches with the late Gus Oliver. It would be good if he were able to exonerate most of them. At the moment, between Oliver's now reduced harem, their partners, his unhappy daughter and his business rivals, Casey still had far too large a load of suspects for comfort.

The first on his list was a Mr Patterson of Kincaid and Co. Like Oliver, he too had his offices on the industrial estate. Kincaid's was a smaller concern than Gus Oliver's to judge from the size of the building, but like the others on the list, according to Caroline Everett they and the other firms dealt in the same line and were forever trying to undercut one another with their suppliers or nobble each other in some other way.

Mr Patterson turned out to be a tall, well-muscled man if his handshake was anything to go by. He didn't seem worried about the reason for Casey's visit, which Casey had explained to him over the phone. In fact he was quite welcoming and jovial in his manner.

'Come in, Chief Inspector, come in. Sit down,' he invited. 'I gather from my secretary that you're here about Gus Oliver's murder?'

'That's right, sir. I'm currently checking into his movements and those of any acquaintances.'

Patterson nodded. 'I supposed that's why you wanted to see me. Given my various court battles with Oliver, I imagine I must be a prime suspect?'

Casey kept a discreet silence.

'I gather from the newspapers that he was found in an alleyway here in King's Langley early on Monday morning?'

Casey nodded, but said nothing more.

'Well now, let me see.' He stared off into space in recollection, then nodding as if in remembrance of the day, he turned back to Casey and said, 'I had a late start that day and was still at home with my wife till gone nine. Check with her if you like.' He rattled off his address and phone number.

'And what about Friday evening around nine and into the early hours of Saturday morning, which is the time we believe Mr Oliver to have been killed? Perhaps you could tell me where you were between those hours.'

'Certainly. I was again at home with my wife. There were again just the two of us, I'm afraid.' He shrugged and stood up, adding a little joke: 'Hope she's good for the alibi.'

And suddenly he became very businesslike, all joviality vanishing. It was as if he wanted to make clear what a busy man he was and even murders of business rivals mustn't hold him up.

'Now, if that's all, I have a very full day ahead of me. I don't see why I should allow the dead Oliver to disrupt my day any more than the live one did.'

Casey nodded and allowed himself to be ushered out. He would take a harder line if Mrs Patterson failed to corroborate her husband's story.

The other three rival businessmen with whom Oliver had been embroiled in court battles all turned out to have firm alibis, being at the same conference in the Midlands. The information they supplied was soon checked out. It felt good to be able to cross some more names off their now diminishing list of suspects.

After another day of full-on checking and eliminating, Casey called the team to the incident room for a well-deserved pat on the back.

'You'll be glad to know that, of the suspects known

to the dead man and who might have reason to want to kill him, because of your hard work we've eliminated many and these suspects are now reduced to nine in number.'

'Unless some more ladies come out of the woodwork,' Catt pointed out from where he was propped against the wall combing his hair. 'And always supposing it wasn't a stranger murder – a mugging gone wrong.' Catt always liked to look his best, but his fiddling with his comb was a bone of contention between him and Casey. However, for now, Casey ignored it.

'Yes, we're still not able to discount that possibility, though given that the pathologist has confirmed the victim was moved after death, that seems increasingly unlikely. Anyway, to get back to what I was saying, Mrs Alice Oliver, the victim's wife, who readily admitted she knew of his serial infidelities, is one of our suspects. As are Amanda and Roger Meredith, Sarah and Carl Garrett and Max Fallon and his live-in partner, Carole Brown, all of whom are numbered amongst his lovers and their partners. Like Mrs Oliver, Fallon and Carole Brown only live around the corner from the alleyway where Oliver was found. Max Fallon, Carole Brown's partner, is obsessively jealous according to what Catt found out from the neighbours. He had apparently supposedly learned about his girlfriend's affair only a few days before Oliver's death. He's had a few run-ins with us but little has come to anything.'

'Another indicator of possible guilt is the fact that Ms Brown claims she and the dead man were going to leave their respective partners and set up home together,' Catt put in. 'She rang up earlier with this titbit,' he told Casey. 'Wonder if she thought it a good excuse to take her out of the running? If this Max Fallon found that out also—'

'Quite,' Casey broke in. 'Always supposing it's true. It doesn't sound likely, given that Mrs Oliver claims her husband was commitment phobic.'

'Maybe, as Catt said, it's just a crude attempt on Carole Brown's part to make us believe she had no reason to kill him?' Constable Jonathon Keane put in from the back of the room.

'Maybe,' Casey said. 'Certainly, we found nothing at either Mr Oliver's home or his business premises to indicate he had plans for a new life with Carole Brown or anyone else.

'Max Fallon is something of a ne'er-do-well. He has criminal associates and is known for being violent. There are rumours from Sergeant Catt's sources that a knife is his weapon of preference. Carole Brown is much younger than Fallon and reputedly flirtatious. We've yet to question any of these men as to their whereabouts when Gus Oliver was killed, though Mr Meredith was, according to his wife, at home at the time and working in his office at the top of the house.

'Then there's Mr Patterson of Kincaid's. The only person he was able to produce to confirm his whereabouts was his wife, though we've yet to question his neighbours. One of them might have noticed him going out. Lastly, we have Caitlin Osborne, the victim's illegitimate daughter. When we questioned Mrs Oliver about the identity of anyone else with a possible grudge against her husband, she mentioned the girl and that Oliver had refused all attempts by his daughter to have a relationship. The daughter sounds a troubled girl. She's apparently left her adoptive parents' home in Liverpool during the last few weeks and is now alone in the world and probably nursed a grudge against her father. She's a known drug user and has been in and out of prison for the last few years owing to thefts she used to support her drug-taking. She has also been sectioned in psychiatric hospitals several times as she suffered some psychotic episodes. We've still trying to trace her, but it's possible she travelled to King's Langley to make one last ditch attempt to persuade her father to let her into his life.'

'Or to remove him from it permanently,' Catt put in. 'Maybe the method of murder was symbolic,' he suggested. 'Maybe, if Cally the scally was the one who cut off her father's tackle, she was ensuring, in some way that appealed to her crazed mental state, that he couldn't father any more unwanted children. It could be the kind of violent action that would appeal to the psychotic mind.'

'And not just the psychotic mind,' Casey quietly pointed out. 'This was a man, remember, who went in for sexual betrayal on the grand opera scale. Any one of his lovers who have failed to provide sustainable alibis might have been tempted to emasculate him, once they discovered they were merely one in a long line of convenient females. So might their various partners.'

He paused and glanced at Catt. 'As to the other possibility – that he was killed by a mugger – since the post-mortem results, as I said, that's looking less likely, as the victim didn't die in that alley as was originally thought possible. His body was clearly moved after death, as Dr Merriman makes clear in his report on the hypostasis – the blood that sinks to the lowest extremities after death,' he explained for the benefit of the younger members of the team whose experience of death was limited.

'Muggers tend to have more interest in fleeing the scene of their crime than in concealing the body of their victim, so I suggest we concentrate our efforts on digging deeper into those known to the victim and who lack an alibi: his wife; his three unalibied lovers; their partners; Mr Patterson; and the victim's daughter, Caitlin Osborne.'

'There's still the fact that his wallet was missing,' Catt pointed out, like a dog after a particularly juicy bone. As so often, he had chosen to play the role of devil's advocate.

Casey nodded. 'I hadn't forgotten. But as I said, his killer could have taken it simply in an attempt to delay any identification. The mutilation could have been done to muddy the waters. We really can't afford to discount anything at this stage, but for now I'd like to concentrate our efforts. Time enough to cast our net wider if the more likely suspects prove innocent of this crime.

'Right,' he said, 'let's get moving. I want our suspects' friends, neighbours and family questioned again. The suspects themselves will be firmly questioned, too, of course. Sergeant Catt and I will take on that role. The rest of you, closely question everyone else – you can sort out the details between you. I want to know any gossip you can extract, indications of temperament and, given the level of violence perpetrated against the victim, anyone else, apart from Fallon, with an inclination to violence.

'Although only one of our suspects has a criminal record – Fallon, the nightclub proprietor – ask around to discover if any of them have a reputation amongst their neighbours for aggression. Most people, in my experience, unless they have mental health issues, tend to build up to the kind of violence that was used here. They don't just start at this kind of level, not even nowadays with the rising levels of gratuitous violence in modern society. OK. Off you go.'

As the team filed out, Casey glanced at his watch. It was approaching the time for him to ring his mother to find out if there had been any developments at the smallholding that ThomCatt's Lincolnshire police friend hadn't already confided.

He nodded at Catt and tapped his mobile. Catt didn't fail to understand the significance of the gesture, as his immediate grin confirmed. 'I'll wait in the car,' he said. 'Remember me to your parents.'

As soon as Catt had left, scared of prying ears, Casey removed himself from the confines of the police station to the street around the corner to make his call. He found an empty doorway and rang Moon, praying that the murders in her midst would have encouraged a degree more responsibility than she had ever previously displayed. It was important to find out what interactions and revelations had gone on between the commune members when they were on their own. They could just yet prove revealing.

To Casey's surprise, his mother answered her mobile on only the sixth ring: a veritable model of efficiency for her.

'Willow Tree, hon. I almost forgot you were ringing. What time is it?'

'It's seven o'clock, Mum. The time I arranged I'd ring you.' Although Casey did his best to keep disapproval from his voice, from his mother's reply it was clear he hadn't entirely succeeded.

'Don't hassle me, son. There's been enough hassle here to last me and Star through any number of karmic incarnations.'

'And will be until DCI Boxham finds out who killed your friends,' Casey reminded her, in the hope that it would incline her to face up to the reality that she and Star were witnesses – *suspects* Casey reluctantly corrected himself – in a double murder inquiry. And that the sooner they provided him with some evidence that pointed to one of the other commune members being the murderer, the sooner the hassle would stop. 'So tell me, what's been happening?'

'Like I said, hassle, man. Accusations. More arguments. Jethro's started most of them.'

Jethro Redfern, Casey recalled, was the brother of the pregnant Madonna and the teenage son of Lilith and Foxy Redfern – unless, that was, the evidence of his own eyes that he bore a marked resemblance to Star Casey meant he was his own half sibling.

'That boy's got so much anger in him,' Moon complained. 'I said to him, "Stay cool. Chill out. Smoke some weed," but he wouldn't listen.'

Good for Jethro, Casey thought. 'So what were these arguments about?'

'Apart from these two deaths, it was the usual stuff. He was hassling his father for not taking better care of his daughter; hassling Kali Callender because it was her old man who got his sister pregnant.'

'Why did the boy blame Mrs Callender for the fact her husband made Madonna pregnant?'

'He seemed to think Kali should have been able to control her husband.' Moon laughed. 'Kid's got a lot to learn.'

'Anything else?'

There was a silence on the other end of the line. It lasted all of ten seconds, then Moon said, 'The commune has a real bad aura now, Willow Tree. It's not the same place at all.'

As far as Casey was concerned the commune had always

had a bad aura. It didn't smell too sweet, either, but he let
the comment pass.

'Some of the others are talking of moving on.'

'That would be very foolish,' Casey warned. There was
no one else to try to stop them doing something stupid
that would, to suspicious police minds, be as indicative
of guilt as running away. 'Tell me you and Star aren't
thinking of joining this would-be band of travelling
hippies.'

'Hey, Willow Tree, I'm not stupid, you know. Besides,
Star's got no appetite any more for a life on the road, moving
from place to place. He likes the creature comforts of the
commune. Don't worry, hon, we're staying put.'

Casey was glad to hear it, not relishing a manhunt for
the pair, though he smiled as he thought of the 'creature
comforts' of their dilapidated and much neglected smallholding. It was as well that Star was easily pleased. 'Good.
Make sure you do. Doing a flit would concentrate DCI
Boxham's eye quicker than an eagle on a rabbit. Let the
others run away if they must.' He paused. 'So who was it,
exactly, who was so keen to leave?'

'Oh, I don't know. They were all talking at once, so it
wasn't clear, though I think Foxy Redfern would have gone
like a shot, only Madonna's near her time and not feeling
well and when he suggested they leave, she started to cry.
That caused another row between Foxy and Lilith,
Madonna's mum.'

'Any others who said they wanted to leave?'

'Young Randy wanted to go. He's a sensitive soul. But
Scott talked him out of it. He said that, with them both
being gay, neither of them had any argument with DaisyMay.
And it's true, they didn't have any. We all know one another's
business in the commune. And another thing, you wouldn't
believe how much they were looking forward to the two
babies being born. Madonna's and DaisyMay's. Randy even
taught himself to knit and made the most fab sets of booties.
So cute.'

There wasn't much of anything to help solve the case
amongst what Moon had told him, Casey realized. So he

probed deeper. 'You said there were accusations bandied about,' he reminded her.

'Did I?' Moon asked, her voice so vague, that Casey suspected he would be lucky to have his question answered.

'Come on, Mum. Try to think. You're my only source of information.' This last wasn't strictly true, of course. He had ThomCatt's channel into the Lincolnshire force. Not that he was about to confide that to Moon. Thomas Catt was already risking a lot to help him and his parents; he wasn't willing to have him put further at risk by letting Moon know of his involvement.

'Help me here, Mum. Try to remember. If I'm to help you and Star, I need you to help me. And for you to do that, I need you to keep your wits about you. It might be an idea to lay off the weed,' he suggested. And whatever other noxious substances she took.

'Lay off the weed?' For once, his usually laidback mother sounded put out. But then a combination of being a murder suspect and being asked to give up a favourite vice would be likely to do that to a person. 'I've got no choice about that, have I? The pigs not only took the growing plants, they took my private stash too. And everyone else's. I won't have any money to buy more till my pension comes. I don't suppose . . .' she began, in a wheedling voice.

'You don't suppose right,' Casey told her firmly. 'Anyway, what about the money from your lottery win? Surely you haven't gone through that already?'

When there was no answer to this, he added firmly, 'I want you to have a clear head.' Or as clear as it ever got, anyway. 'Now about those accusations you mentioned—'

'I told you,' she said flatly, 'I forget what they were about. Something and nothing, probably.'

Exasperated, Casey for the moment admitted defeat. Before he bid his mother goodnight, he reminded her again to conceal the mobile somewhere safe and away from the house. 'I'll ring you at the same time tomorrow evening. Seven o'clock,' he reminded her. 'Don't forget.'

'Yeah, yeah, I know.'

The phone went dead. She hadn't even said goodnight, which was unlike the generally good-natured Moon. And if the situation at the commune was getting under *her* skin, it showed how bad it must be.

Ten

Casey dropped his mobile into his pocket and returned to the back entrance to the police station and the car park where Catt was waiting for him. He was hopeful that this evening would move them further forward. And even though their unofficial inquiry was making small progress and receiving little assistance to help him extract his parents from their self-induced difficulties, he couldn't afford to let it make him neglect the Oliver investigation.

'So, what did your mother have to say when you spoke to her?' Catt asked as Casey climbed in to the passenger seat.

'Very little. And none of it much help. Though she did say there have been plenty of rows amongst the commune members.'

'Brotherly love: it was ever thus,' Catt intoned. 'Though that's hardly surprising in the circumstances with a double murder hanging over their stoned heads.'

'True.' Casey fastened his seat belt while Catt manoeuvred the car out of the yard and on to the road, before he pointed the bonnet towards the park and Mrs Oliver's home.

Casey was wary of letting ThomCatt know just how little cooperation he was getting from Moon. He might just conclude that if she couldn't be bothered to make some effort on her own behalf, why should he trouble to try to help them.

Casey wouldn't blame him if he did come to such a conclusion. It was a conclusion that his own mind had played with intermittently. But, as he couldn't afford to have his limited posse of helpers diminish to nothing, he kept his mouth firmly closed and concentrated on reading over his notes

prior to re-interviewing Mrs Oliver. It provided him with
an excuse for his silence.

When they arrived at Mrs Oliver's house, a lorry was backing
in to the drive. It was piled with rolls of new turf.

After they had edged their way past the press pack
crowding the gates, Catt glanced at Casey and raised his
eyebrows as he parked up. 'Strange thing for a supposedly
grieving widow to get the garden re-laid at such a time.'

'Probably forgot all about it until the men turned up. I
had my turf re-laid last year and I had to order it in advance.
I imagine Mrs Oliver didn't feel up to the likely row if she
cancelled the job.'

Catt shrugged and climbed from the car.

They watched as the gardeners heaved the rolls of turf
on to their shoulders and made for the side gate. The last
of the three-man band – presumably the foreman – carried
just a green tarpaulin.

Casey called to him, 'A bit late for gardening work.'

'Yeah. We're running late. We're just dumping the turf for
now and will set to and lay it in the morning.' He disappeared
through the gate after the other men. They were quickly back
and all three piled into the lorry and headed off.

Shazia Khan, the female officer whom Casey had left
behind with Mrs Oliver to fend off reporters, had since been
relieved and, after he'd had a few words with her replace-
ment, Casey made for the drawing room, knocked on the
door and entered at the 'Come in' invitation.

Mrs Oliver didn't look as well-groomed as she had on
their previous visit. Understandable if the effort required to
make herself presentable was too much. As Casey knew,
many of the recently bereaved let themselves go for a time.
Her eyes were red-rimmed, too, he noticed. The reality of
her husband's death was clearly sinking in. She seemed
brittle, with a distant air about her as if she wasn't really
taking much notice of anything any longer.

'I'm sorry to bother you again so soon, Mrs Oliver,' Casey
began once they were seated in the over-heated drawing
room.

She came out of her reverie to say in a firm voice, 'Don't be, Chief Inspector. You must "bother" me, as you call it, as often as you need. As Gus's wife—' she grimaced and broke off before she corrected herself. 'As Gus's *widow*, I understand you have a job to do. I expect nothing less and neither would Gus.' She found a shadowy smile and added, 'Gus would probably haunt me if I let you get away with a less than rigorous investigation into his death. And rightly so.'

Casey inclined his head in acknowledgement. 'It's just a few more questions and then we'll leave you in peace. If you're sure you feel ready to answer them?'

'I'm ready. What is it you want to know?'

'You said you last saw your husband around nine o'clock on Friday night?'

She nodded. 'Give or take ten minutes or so.'

'I also understand that it was his custom to stay away from home for one or two nights on a regular basis?'

'As you have discovered, Chief Inspector, my husband was a law unto himself. He never liked me to question him about his movements. I suppose, over the years, he's trained me not to do so. I learned the lesson well.'

'So I don't suppose he gave any indication as to where he was going?'

'No. You asked me that before,' she said sharply. So she wasn't in quite such a faraway place as he had thought. 'Apart from saying it was some business meeting.' She forced a smile. 'But then he always said that. It didn't make it true, as I have discovered.'

'Strange time for a business meeting,' Catt remarked, 'even if that was just an excuse for meeting one of his lady friends.'

'Quite. As I imagine your inquiries will reveal, his appointment that evening was unlikely to have been of a business nature. Gus had the ability to trot out excuses as well as any confidence trickster.'

Casey let her answer slide past him, but he continued his questions on the same theme. 'I get the impression that Mr Oliver was in the habit of going out on his own in the evenings quite frequently.' Smoothly, Casey resumed. 'You didn't mind?'

'Over the years we evolved our own interests. Once I would have minded that he liked going out without me, but those days are long gone. Besides, I wouldn't have wanted to play gooseberry while he romanced his latest woman. I suppose you can say we slipped into a routine, one that suited both of us to a degree. Gus has always been gregarious; he thought an evening wasted if he wasn't socializing. I'm rather reserved and not keen on social gatherings so we compromised. As long as I accompanied him to important functions he was happy for me to stay home the rest of the time.'

'Still, it must have been lonely for you here on your own, night after night.'

'Not really. I'm quite a self-contained woman. And, as I said, I have my own interests.'

Casey paused briefly before he returned to the painful subject of her husband's infidelities. 'You said that you knew about your husband's affairs and accepted them.'

She nodded. 'I can see that it must seem a strange thing for a wife to accept. But it has been the normal thing in our marriage for many years now. Gus was a very –' she hesitated before selecting the word – 'athletic man. Very physical. Whereas I have always been more inclined to cerebral pursuits.' She gave a tiny shrug. 'I suppose, in that way, we were ill-matched.' She nodded towards the floor to ceiling bookcases that lined the fireplace walls at both ends of the large room. The shelves were so tight-packed that it would be only with difficulty that one would be able to prise a book from the clutch of its neighbours.

A quick glance over some of the titles certainly indicated that their owner had an intellectual inclination. There was little fiction, Casey saw, but there were shelves on sociology and psychology, which Mrs Oliver explained she had studied at university.

She had gone to Durham, which, she told them, was where she had met her husband.

'It was quite a surprise for his crowd when we got

together.' She gave a short laugh. 'I confess, it was quite a surprise to me, too. Gus was, I suppose, what is nowadays termed an "Alpha Male", even when he was young.'

Casey nodded, then drew her back to the point. 'We have reason to believe your husband died some time on the evening he left here; before midnight rather than after. He certainly didn't die in that alley.' Dr Merriman had been quite clear on this point. 'It's plain that someone took a risk in moving him. I'm afraid I have to ask everyone where they were from nine on the Friday evening to around midnight and from six to seven thirty on Monday morning, between which hours we have reason to believe he was dumped in the alley.'

She looked shocked to be asked such a question. But then she nodded slowly, as if accepting his right to ask it of her. 'I was at home during both relevant times, Chief Inspector. On the Friday evening I was alone, but as far as the Monday goes, I suppose I have a witness. Mrs Clarke, Mrs Mary Clarke, my cleaning lady was here.'

'I see. What time did she start work?'

'She was here just before six and worked for three hours. She's an early bird, like me, and likes to get started on her chores as soon in the day as possible. We're a perfect match in that way and I fit in nicely with her more lie-abed customers. She always starts her working day here and then goes on to clean the houses of the lie-abeds afterwards. She has her own key so can let herself in without disturbing me if I'm busy.'

Once he had obtained the cleaning lady's address, Casey decided to leave it there. He would question this Mrs Clarke and get her version of events for the Monday morning when Gus Oliver's body was found. But if she confirmed that Alice Oliver was at home when she arrived and didn't leave the house during the following hour and a half it looked like Mrs Oliver was in the clear – at least as far as dumping the body was concerned. And as it seemed certain that Oliver was murdered and later dumped by the same person, that would appear to exonerate her from both.

But, he reflected, as he stood up, thanked her for her

time and followed Catt out, they still had enough other potential suspects to keep them busy.

Mrs Clarke, Alice Oliver's cleaning lady, lived in a tiny terraced house about five minutes' walk away from Alice Oliver. She confirmed what Mrs Oliver had told them. The house was as neat as a newly planted flowerbed, with a place for everything and everything in its place. It certainly seemed to sum up Mary Clarke's attitude to housework.

She was a stout woman, over retirement age and looking it, with work-worn hands and a vaguely resentful manner.

As they followed her along the short, narrow hall to the back kitchen, Casey asked, 'Have you worked for Mrs Oliver for long?'

She invited them to sit, her lips pursing slightly as she watched the two big policemen as if annoyed at how untidy they made her very clean and well-scrubbed kitchen. 'I suppose you want tea?' she asked.

They both nodded and thanked her as she turned away to fill the kettle.

'I've worked for Mrs Oliver for coming up three years now. Since just before I was divorced,' she told them as she crossed to the fridge and took the milk out. It was in a much polished silver jug, which she placed on the table before bringing out the sugar. 'A very nice lady, Mrs Oliver, very considerate.'

She made the tea and brought it and fine bone china cups and saucers to the table before she sat down. She had said nothing about Gus Oliver, Casey noticed, but then, he supposed she could rarely have seen the man during her working hours as she went on to reveal that Gus Oliver had generally had a working breakfast in his study, which his wife prepared and where he was not to be disturbed.

'You got on well with Mrs Oliver. How about Mr Oliver? I know you said you saw little of him, but you must have gained some impression.'

Mrs Clarke sniffed, stirred the pot and poured the tea. 'It's not for me to speak ill of the dead. I cleaned for them, that's all. I wasn't invited to their dinner parties. As long

as I was left to get on with my work without interference
– and I was – we generally got along just fine.' She reached
for a washing-up sponge from the sink tidy and ran it over
the table where Catt had spilled a few drops of tea from
his dainty cup, before she added, 'I like my routines, Chief
Inspector. I don't like them upset. Mrs Oliver understands
that. Not like some of my ladies.'

'And Mr Oliver?'

'As I said, I didn't see much of him. He didn't interfere,
if that's what you mean.'

She seemed reluctant to discuss Gus Oliver. Perhaps she
hadn't liked the man and given her quoted adage about not
liking to speak ill of the dead, she preferred to say as little
as possible. If there was any ill-speaking due it was clear
that Mrs Clarke didn't intend to break her silence on the
matter, even if her manner spoke volumes.

'You saw Mrs Oliver on Monday morning?'

'Oh yes. She was up when I arrived just before six. I
was in the kitchen giving the cupboards a good clean out.
I could hear her computer printing out. It's rather an old-
fashioned one and makes quite a bit of noise. Like me, Mrs
Oliver is a lady who dislikes wasting time. She keeps herself
very busy. Unsurprising, of course, with—' she broke off
abruptly before she said anything incriminating.

Had she been going to say 'with a husband like him'?
Casey wondered.

'You saw her? You didn't just hear her printer?'

'Of course I saw her.' Mrs Clarke bridled at the question. 'You surely can't suspect Mrs Oliver of murder? She's
a fine lady. Besides, she came downstairs about seven
o'clock and made us both some tea. She didn't go out. I'd
have seen her as the kitchen faces the front door and the
back door is in the kitchen. I can see the whole of the back
garden from there so I would have seen her if she'd gone
out through the patio doors in the lounge.' She sat back,
with an expression that said 'Make something of *that* if
you can' etched clearly on her face.

That let Alice Oliver pretty well off the hook when it
came to dumping the body, Casey acknowledged. According

to Cedric Abernethy, there had been no body in the alley when he had left home to walk the dog just before six on Monday morning.

'We'll need you to come to the station to make a formal statement,' he told her.

'When? Only, as I told you, I have my routines. My days are pretty full with all my ladies. If I'm late getting to one it will throw my entire day out.'

'Fit it in at a time to suit you. Let us know when and we can send a car to collect you.'

'That won't be necessary. I have my own car. I learned to drive after my husband left me. It's only a cheap little runabout, but it does me. Now –' she glanced at the clock on the wall – 'I need to get on. I promised Mrs Townsend that I'd give her spare room a good do before her visitors arrive and I'm keen to get on with it.'

She followed them out and bustled hurriedly off to her car.

'Amazing what some people can get enthusiastic about,' Catt remarked as they climbed in to their own car. 'Would you ever feel that eager to sort out a spare room? Particularly one that wasn't even your own?'

Casey smiled. And although he liked a tidy home – a trait clearly not inherited from his parents – he said, 'I can think of other pursuits that would be more welcome. But her evidence seems pretty conclusive, so that's one suspect down and seven to go. By the way, I was going to ask you if you've had any more news from your friend on the Lincolnshire force.'

'Yeah. I texted him while you were on the phone to your parents.' Catt put the car into gear and pulled away from the kerb. 'Meant to tell you. Anyway, that couple, Honey and Ché Farrer, who left your parents' smallholding a while back, are out of the running for DaisyMay's murder at least. They both have rock-solid alibis. So even if they can't recall exactly where they were or what they were doing around the time we've roughly estimated that Kris Callender died – and, surprise, surprise, they claim to have left before it occurred – it seems unlikely they had anything to do with that killing either, seeing as you're convinced the two deaths are connected.'

Casey wasn't convinced of that, not completely, though it seemed most likely. But for two murders to occur within a few months of each other and amongst such a small circle seemed too much of a coincidence for them not to be connected.

'Thanks, ThomCatt. You do know how much I appreciate your input on this, don't you?'

Concentrating on the road ahead, Casey sensed rather than saw Catt's grin.

'That's all right, boss. Don't sweat it. Maybe you can do the same for me one day?'

That didn't seem likely. As an orphan, Thomas Catt had been spared the parental traumas that currently rocked Casey's world.

When Casey rang Moon the next evening, she reported that all the police had now departed. 'Even the runty young one they had posted at the gate.'

'You're sure?' Casey questioned. 'There's not any still lingering in one of the back lanes to watch the comings and goings?'

'No. I sent one of the boys out on his bike to scout around. They've definitely gone.'

'In that case, maybe it would be a good time for me to pay another visit. I need to speak to everyone again; maybe a few memories and tongues will have loosened in the interim. I won't arrive till fairly late, as I have another couple of interviews on the Oliver murder to fit in before I can drive up to your place.' The first was with Roger and Amanda Meredith – Amanda being another of Gus Oliver's multiplicity of lovers. 'I should be with you some time after ten.' He paused, then asked, 'Have there been any further developments?'

'There's been no more murders, if that's what you mean.'

That hadn't been Casey's meaning, but he was relieved to hear it all the same.

'How did Star bear up during the questioning?' He'd already asked this question several times, but Moon was patient with him and simply repeated what she'd already told him.

'He didn't let anything slip. But you know Star, with a memory as poor as his, he wouldn't have been able to even if he'd wanted to.'

That was true. Casey let the knowledge comfort him. If Star managed to complete a sentence more than a few words long it would be the first time in several years.

'Anyway, I'll say goodnight for now. Just don't let anything slip that you haven't already told the police. And make sure Star knows he's to say as little as possible if – *when* – the police return.'

'You said. You worry too much, Willow Tree. I've already told you we don't know anything about Kris or DaisyMay's deaths, so we can't say anything.'

As reassured as he was likely to be, Casey bade his mother a second goodnight, reminded her he'd see her later and ended the call.

Eleven

Like an onion, King's Langley was made up of a number of layers, with the medieval centre, then the odd Tudor merchant's house and Georgian rows beyond them and then the Victorian terraces. The Merediths' house was situated on the more leafy outskirts of the town, where space was at less of a premium.

They lived in some splendour. Theirs was a detached Edwardian house, set in spacious grounds which contained a garage that looked large enough to accommodate four cars, as well as other assorted outbuildings. One of these was a stable; the head of an inquisitive chestnut horse stared disdainfully at them over the door.

'Snooty looking bugger. Wonder what he thinks he's got that makes him look down his nose at us,' Catt complained.

'Centuries of breeding, probably.'

'I was *bred*. We were all bred,' Catt pointed out. 'Though I suppose *his* mum stayed around long enough to bring him up, unlike mine. Probably just as well mine buggered off if that's what having a mum around does to your expression.'

'Forget the horse, ThomCatt, and concentrate your mind on the interviews.'

According to what Catt had learned when he had questioned Mrs Meredith, her husband worked as a self-employed consultant in the financial services industry. To judge from the house, it was a profitable line.

'Nice work if you can get it, hey?' said Catt. 'This pair have a lot to lose if one or both of them turn out to be Oliver's murderer. Reckon we can expect a few porkies here.'

Mrs Meredith, who answered the door, turned out to be

small, blonde, dainty and very feminine. Casey, for whom this was the first meeting with any of Oliver's lovers, wondered if she was the type Gus Oliver normally went for. Oliver's wife was a far cry from Amanda Meredith, being tall and edging into plumpness. She was also rather plain, but she was transformed when she smiled. Perhaps, in their early days together, Oliver had made her smile a lot.

Mrs Meredith led them into a drawing room that ran the whole length of the house. It was furnished in an ultra-feminine style, with lots of flounces on the chintz armchairs and settees. Altogether, it was a bit overpowering. Casey found himself wondering how her husband stood it. Perhaps, to compensate, he kept his study at the top of the house austerely masculine.

'Please sit down, gentlemen. I've called my husband down from his office and he'll be with us presently. Can I get you some tea? Or coffee?'

They both refused the tea. This seemed to put her out a little as if she had wanted to play hostess to policemen as an antidote to the frills that surrounded her every day. However, put out or not at their refusal of her offer, she remained polite.

Amanda Meredith's voice had a little girl, breathless quality as her words tumbled out, which Casey found irritating. He thought grown women should behave and speak like adults, not pseudo-adolescents; but perhaps his own parents' refusal to leave their sixties youth behind went a long way to explaining his irritation. Like Moon, Amanda Meredith retained the hairstyle of her girlhood and a blue Alice band held back the curly, naturally blonde locks which looked as if they and their owner spent every spare minute at the hairdresser's – when, that was, she wasn't riding the disdainful stallion. She was altogether a pampered-looking piece, the Alice band giving her a childish look that would hold an appeal for some men.

As with the Olivers, in the Merediths' case, too, opposites had attracted, Casey noted as Roger Meredith entered the room to his wife's twitter of welcome. Meredith was tall and rugged with a businesslike air. From the look of his nose and damaged ears, he had been a rugby player in his youth.

'Chief Inspector,' Roger Meredith, far from coy and gushing like his wife, now asked, 'I understand from your sergeant that you wanted to question my wife and myself about the death of Gus Oliver. Tragic business,' he put in *en passant*, though from his manner as he sat and sank into the depths of one of the frilly armchairs, he didn't seem terribly cut up about Oliver's death. 'I knew him, of course – we both did, though it was a casual acquaintance only. We belong to the same rugby club and we'd occasionally see him there.'

Casey wondered if Roger Meredith was aware that his wife's acquaintance with Gus Oliver was rather more than casual. That was, if their supposition had been correct. She had been cagey both when she had telephoned the incident room to identify Oliver and when Catt had called to question her, so was clearly capable of acting the adult when she chose. If so, Meredith was hiding any suspicion well. But Casey sensed a tension in him that he felt wasn't simply to do with receiving a visit from the police. It would be interesting to learn if he was able to produce an alibi that was an improvement on the one already supplied.

'Has my wife offered you a drink?'

Casey confirmed that she had and again declined any refreshments.

'I'm sure we'll be able to clear this matter up,' Meredith announced firmly.

Casey was sitting on one of the flouncy settees and Catt had chosen an armchair further back from the intimate circle, all the better to view the expressions of their interviewees while keeping a discreet distance.

'My wife tells me you're asking all Gus Oliver's friends and acquaintances if they're able to supply any information. I will, of course, be glad to help in any way I can. I understand the times you're interested in are from around nine to midnight on the Friday and from six-ish to around seven thirty on Monday?'

Casey nodded.

'Well now, let me see . . .' Meredith frowned in thought. 'I left home at half past six on the Friday for a rugby committee meeting.'

'And what time did this meeting end?'

'Eight thirty or thereabouts.'

'And did you come straight home afterwards?'

'No. I stayed on for a couple of drinks. Normally I'd still be there at eleven o'clock, but there were things I wanted to do in my office here at the house, so I didn't linger long. I was at home in my office upstairs from just before nine, wasn't I darling?' he asked his wife.

Amanda Meredith nodded, quick to back up what her husband said.

Did these 'things' that Meredith said he had been doing include catching his wife in flagrante delicto? Casey wondered. Was Roger Meredith aware that his wife had been having an affair with Oliver? Or was he the innocent caught in the middle? And if he had come home unexpectedly early and caught his wife and her lover in bed together, what would he do? Had a red mist descended, resulting in Oliver's death? It was certainly a believable scenario. He could have recognized Oliver's car and, if he already had reasons for suspicion, could have armed himself with a sharp knife before ascending to the bedroom. But if that had happened, Oliver's blood would be everywhere and he doubted that Meredith would be so foolish as to commit such a messy murder. Certainly not in a place from where the mess couldn't be easily got rid of.

But, he remonstrated silently with himself, he was rushing ahead of the facts. 'And you, Mrs Meredith?' he asked. 'I understand from my sergeant that you were at home between the relevant times on both occasions?'

'Yes, that's so,' she replied in her breathy voice. She curled one of her blonde locks around her fingers as she continued. 'Occasionally, I accompany my husband to the rugby club, for lunches, dinners and so on. Committee meetings aren't my style, but I sometimes attend and stay in the bar till the meeting's finished.'

Flirting with any available male, Casey surmised as he

caught her giving him the once-over. She was flirting with him under her husband's nose in spite of being a murder suspect. Her shapely legs were crossed provocatively and her white dress had ridden up to give a glimpse of thigh.

Catt at least seemed to enjoy the view, but Casey found this deliberate attempt to distract them less than appealing. Was it something she did automatically when males were present? Or was it a display she had put on especially for them in order to distract them from their purpose?

'And what about Monday?' he asked Meredith. 'The early morning on Monday?' This was when Cedric Abernethy's evidence indicated that Oliver' body had been dumped in the alley.

'We were both in bed, Chief Inspector,' Meredith responded firmly. He glanced at his wife as he added, 'Sleeping the sleep of the self-righteous.'

At the moment, Casey wasn't in a position to contradict either of their statements. But he obtained the name and location of the rugby club and the names and addresses of the other committee members before he and Catt took their leave.

Catt had arranged for them to see Sarah and Carl Garrett next. They lived clear across town. It seemed that Oliver had liked the members of his harem to live as far apart as convenience warranted but still convenient to visit.

The Garretts lived in a spacious loft apartment over-looking the river. In its way, it must be as pricey as the detached home of the Merediths, providing, as several prominent signs in the entrance hall proclaimed, a gym and swimming pool in the basement as well as a resident porter. The porter would have to be questioned.

The Garretts' second-floor apartment was starkly modern, with sleek, black leather settees and satiny pale blond wood flooring. They had a selection of expensive electrical gadgets, including a huge plasma television.

Sarah Garrett was another dainty, natural blonde. It seemed that Oliver didn't believe in ringing the changes in his lovers, though at least Mrs Garrett wasn't a gushing woman and spoke in normal, adult tones. In fact, she seemed rather distant and reluctant to say much at all.

'My wife tells me you're investigating the death of a certain Gus Oliver, Chief Inspector,' Carl Garrett said once they were all seated. He, like Roger Meredith, was another athletic looking specimen. 'But for the life of me, I can't see what you think we can tell you. We didn't know the man.'

'You may not, sir,' Casey replied, 'but I believe your wife was acquainted with him.'

'Sarah?' Garrett turned interrogative grey eyes on his wife. 'Is it true? Did you know this man?'

'Only casually.' A defensive note had entered her voice, which, to judge from Garrett's narrowed eyes, he had spotted. 'He belonged to the same tennis club that I joined earlier in the year. I only knew him socially and even so I barely knew him. We'd only exchanged civilities, no more.'

Turning his interrogative gaze from his wife, Garrett directed it back to Casey and said, 'That being the case, Chief Inspector, I can't imagine why you should think we know anything about his death.'

Casey parried. 'Of course I don't think that. Not at the moment, anyway. But if you do, doubtless we'll discover that in due course.' It was clear that Garrett wanted to get rid of them and to question his wife more closely. Well, that could wait; Casey was sure Sarah Garrett would be glad of the delay to give her time to come up with some believable answers.

Sarah Garrett was staring at him with pleading eyes, her distant air quite gone. Casey had no intention of betraying the secret of her affair with Oliver; if either one of the pair had murdered him and they succeeded in proving it, the truth of her relationship with the dead man would come out soon enough. Again, they had only another telephone call to the incident room to indicate that Sarah Garrett was one of Oliver's lovers, but Mrs Garrett didn't know that. No wonder she looked apprehensive. He might, he realized, get more cooperation if she had doubts about him holding his tongue on her illicit union.

He expected Carl Garrett to make difficulties about providing an alibi given his claim that he hadn't known the victim, and so it proved.

'This is ridiculous,' he protested. 'I told you I didn't know the man. Why on earth should I want to kill him?' Then his eyes narrowed and he again gazed speculatively at his wife. 'Unless – unless his relationship with my wife was rather more than casual. Is that what you're trying to imply, Chief Inspector?'

Garrett was a cool customer all right. Was he pretending not to have known of his wife's infidelity and playing guessing games with them?

Sarah broke in to nervous laughter. 'Don't be ridiculous, darling. I told you, I hardly knew the man.' She turned to Casey, 'But I suppose you need an alibi from me?' Casey nodded. 'That would be helpful.'

'As I told your sergeant, I was at home all Friday evening.' She gave another laugh. 'Not much of an alibi, I'm afraid. My husband was working late in his office in town here. I imagine some other member of staff can vouch for him.' She looked enquiringly at her husband.

Finally, Carl Garrett decided to be more helpful. 'Unfortunately not. I was alone in the building. It's my own business,' he explained to Casey, 'so naturally I have my own key to get in and catch up on the work when it warrants it. I was there up till about eleven o'clock Friday night. I had some work I wanted to have cleared for a meeting on Monday so I could leave the weekend free.'

Interesting, thought Casey, as he met Catt's eyes under their slightly raised eyebrows. 'Do you often work late, Mr Garrett?'

'At least three evenings a week,' Mrs Garrett told him in the disgruntled voice of the neglected wife. Was that her excuse for her affair with Oliver?

'When it's your own business you have to put the hours in,' Garrett defended himself. 'I've worked hard to build the business up since I inherited from my father.'

It was clearly an ongoing bone of contention between them.

Casey also found himself wondering whether Carl Garrett used one or more of those evenings playing away rather than working. He questioned them about the early hours of

Monday morning and, like the Merediths, they claimed to have been innocently tucked up in bed.

Having learned what he had come for, Casey eased himself from his seat. 'Thank you for your cooperation.' He glanced in turn from Sarah to her husband. 'We'll see ourselves out.'

'But look here, Chief Inspector,' Carl Garrett protested, 'you can't just leave it like that. What happens now?'

'What happens now?' Casey repeated. Good question. He wished he knew. But he said, 'Now I hope to find sufficient evidence to catch a murderer. Good day to you both.'

His blunt words seemed to deflate Garrett, for he sank back in his chair with an air of defeat, his argumentative streak quite deflated.

After they left the Garretts' apartment, they walked down the stairs and sought out the porter. Red-faced, portly, as befitted his porterly role, and clearly over retirement age, the porter had been stealing forty winks in his little cubbyhole of an office behind the desk. They wakened him with difficulty. It seemed likely he told them the truth when he said he had seen neither of the Garretts on either the Friday night or the Monday morning when his duty shift had changed to earlies.

'Snoring his head off, probably,' said Catt caustically. 'He's a fat lot of use as a witness, anyway.'

Casey nodded. It meant that neither of the Garretts could be exonerated. It also meant that one or both of them would have known there was a good chance they could slip out unnoticed if they needed to. And slip back again.

'Reckon Garrett knew his wife was carrying on with Oliver?' Catt asked when they were back in the car.

'As to that, I don't know. He certainly seemed adamant that *he* didn't know the dead man.' Casey turned the key in the ignition, depressed the clutch and selected first gear before heading for the end of the short drive. 'But one thing's for sure, we've placed a nasty suspicion in his mind about his wife's possible conduct with Oliver. I wonder if he prefers to leave it alone and remain in ignorance or if he'll keep questioning her till he gets the truth.'

'The latter, I suspect, judging from his expression. Unless,' said Catt, 'he already knows the truth and was doing his best to pretend that it was only our visit that had put the idea that she was cheating on him into his head.'

'Mmm, there's always that. Let's hope if he suspects his wife's been having an affair that there's not another murder committed.'

'Amen to that.'

Twelve

It was after nine; too late to call on Max Fallon and Carole Brown as he had hoped. Catt had been unable to speak to either of the couple to make an appointment. Given that Fallon's violent history made him meaty stuff as a suspect, Casey had thought of turning up unexpectedly, hoping to surprise some revelations from one or both of them, but a visit so late in the evening would be more likely to put them on their guard. They would have to wait till tomorrow night. Casey headed back to the station so they could write up the evening's two interviews. Fallon and Ms Brown would wait another day; maybe the wait would rattle them.

The money from their lottery win must have gone to their heads, Casey surmised, for he could see any number of lights blazing from the commune's farmhouse as he approached down the rutted lane. Even with the lights, an air of wretchedness still hung over the place. It was certainly squalid enough for any number of black deeds to have occurred there. Casey wondered if – with the endemic drug-taking – paranoia didn't haunt the place. Had one of the inmates of Paradise Regained, which was what they had named their small plot, gone quietly mad, without the rest noticing?

The possibility wasn't as unlikely as it sounded. When you spent your life in a drug-soaked daze, alertness and noticing things were not strong traits. They might not notice madness in their midst until the paranoid person grabbed a carelessly discarded mallet and let fly with it. And maybe not even then.

The dogs set up their usual cacophony as he stopped at the gate and bipped the horn. As before, Moon came out to unlock the gate and as he slipped through, Casey asked, 'How are things?'

'Much as you'd expect,' she replied with a strange grimness in her tone which more than hinted that Paradise Regained had metamorphosed into purgatory. 'We're all at one another's throats, as I told you last time we spoke,' Moon continued as they walked towards the house. 'Dylan Harper is still keeping to his room. Oh and Billy *has* got mumps. He's keeping to his room as well. The men insist on it.'

Casey nodded. Understandable if Harper was keeping his distance from the rest, especially if he really was grief-stricken: the bedlam created by numerous children, teenagers and dogs that crowded into the commune would hardly be conducive to a person trying to come to terms with the sudden and violent death of a loved one.

Moon glanced at him. 'Reckon he thinks one of us murdered DaisyMay and he's avoiding us as much as he can?'

Did she really expect him to answer that? he wondered. Because, clearly, the answer would have to be 'yes'. Dylan Harper had struck him as a suspicious-minded man, not a natural commune resident at all. On his previous visits he hadn't seemed to mix much with the other members, nor had he appeared to share much in their rough and ready friendships.

But it seemed Moon didn't expect a reply, because she didn't push for one. Instead, she took his arm and led him towards the open farmhouse door.

He stopped her before she entered the house. 'Would you say his grief is genuine, Moon, or put on to allay us thinking that *he* might have killed his wife?'

'What a suspicious mind you have, Willow Tree. His grief seems genuine to me. Not that I've seen much of him since the last time you came here. Besides, why would he kill her? He doted on her. I told you.'

'What about recently? Had his behaviour towards her changed at all?'

'No. In fact, if anything, he became even more attentive since her pregnancy and was so right up to her death. Couldn't do enough for her once she became pregnant. Hardly let her stir out of her chair. They'd been trying for a baby for over a year with no luck. DaisyMay wanted both of them to go for tests, but Dylan wouldn't go.' Moon laughed. 'Just like a man. But, as I said, it ended happily when DaisyMay fell pregnant shortly after. At first he was a bit quiet, but then, once he'd come to terms with the idea that they really were going to have a baby, Dylan was like a cockerel with the loudest crow in the coop. I never saw a man more pleased about being a father.

'It's weird 'cos I'd never had thought Dylan would take so well to the idea in reality. But you never can tell. Funnily enough, it was DaisyMay who seemed to go off the idea almost as soon as she knew she was pregnant. Scared of the birth, I expect, like most women.

'Anyway, as DaisyMay's pregnancy advanced he treated her more and more with kid gloves. It was sweet to see.'

Moon sounded wistful, as well she might; Casey couldn't imagine that his father had treated a Moon pregnant with *him* with such tender care.

Moon's answer didn't please Casey. But, for now, he had no choice but to accept it.

'We're all up before the beak again this week,' she broke the news without preamble. 'Further charges.' She gave a careless shrug. 'I forget what.'

Casey just stopped himself from nodding: this had been one of the things Catt had found out. 'What are you going to plead?'

'Me and Star? Not guilty, of course.'

'Is that sensible? You were all caught red-handed. What does your solicitor say?'

'Oh, him.' With a wave of her be-ringed and henna-decorated hand, Moon dismissed the very expensive solicitor whose services Casey had obtained for his parents. 'He wants us to plead guilty but with diminished responsibility.'

'Sounds sensible.' Certainly in Star's case, though for Moon, Casey doubted even the expensive brief he had hired for the pair would be able to pull it off. She could be sharp when it suited her and she might just show it in the witness box.

'What? You want us to act gaga?'

Casey reflected that, again in Star's case, that wouldn't prove too far a stretch. 'Not gaga, no,' he temporised, 'just easily led, perhaps.'

Moon gave a 'Humph' to that, which might have meant anything. Casey followed her into the farmhouse living room.

The reaction to his reappearance was distinctly hostile from various members of the commune and Casey heard unwelcoming groans from several throats; maybe the Lincolnshire police hadn't treated them with gentle consideration and their behaviour had, in their minds, rubbed off on him, though only Foxy Redfern was belligerent enough to voice their hostility. What had he and the rest expected after trying to conceal two murders?

'Well, look who it ain't,' Redfern drawled as soon as Casey stepped through the door and entered the large and untidy living room. 'The great detective returns. Still not managed to figure out which ne'er-do-well outsider killed DaisyMay and Kris? Surely by now you've found out his dealer's identity?'

'Not yet, Mr Redfern,' Casey replied calmly with an untruth which wasn't a complete lie; he suspected that Callender might have had another supplier other than Tony Magann. Besides, he was determined not to let the man anger him into letting something slip; better to keep him and the rest in the dark and worrying. 'But we're making progress.'

'Progress? Is having our place turned over by the cops what you call "progress"? It's like a nurse describing a patient as "comfortable" when they're anything but.'

'Ruined the entire ambiance of the place,' Moon commented from behind him.

Casey ignored her and addressed Redfern's complaint. 'I'm sorry you feel like that, Mr Redfern, but I hope you can appreciate that I'm doing my best under difficult circumstances.'

'Yes. Leave my Willow Tree alone, Foxy,' Moon broke in, in direct juxtaposition to her previous comment. It was, as ever, all right for Moon to find fault with her son, but she soon flared up when someone else dared to do the same. It was motherly love of a sort, Casey supposed. 'You should be grateful he's taken the case on instead of sniping at him.'

'Let's face it, he's not taken it on for my sake,' Foxy snapped back. 'It's only because of you and Star that he's here at all. Maybe he thinks one of you killed them both and is looking to pin the blame on the rest of us. It wouldn't be the first time a cop has fitted someone up. And why else would he bother trying to find the answer as to who killed DaisyMay and Callender?'

'Now you're being stupid,' Moon told him before Casey could say anything. 'Why should he? If he's anything, my Willow Tree is an honest copper.' She even managed to make it sound as if it was something she admired, which was a first to Casey's recollection.

'Perhaps we should get down to some facts,' Casey broke in before the argument could develop further. He turned to Moon. 'Have you been questioned again by the Lincolnshire force since I spoke to you earlier?'

Moon replied, 'No. I think they want to keep us on tenterhooks by letting us know as little as possible before the court case, though one of the men at a neighbouring farm took great pleasure in telling me the police had questioned him and his wife about us. I told you they're going to take DNA samples from all the men in the commune?'

Casey nodded.

'Well, all the men bar Dylan. He simply refused.'

'Rather foolish of him, seeing as it makes him more interesting to the police.'

'That's what I told him, but he wouldn't listen. Men seldom listen to good sense. God knows why he's being so difficult.'

In contrast to Foxy Redfern, Kali Callender, Kris Callender's widow, had no complaints. She looked pleased with life. Someone, maybe even Kali herself, had removed her unwanted husband, which was, apparently, all right with her. She even attacked Foxy Redfern on Casey's behalf.

'Leave the man alone, Foxy,' she said. 'Surely even you can understand how difficult it is to try to conduct an unofficial investigation? I'm sure he's doing his best for all of us.'

'That's right,' Moon put in. 'My Willow Tree always does his best. It's the way he's made. He can't do anything else. And I think the rest of you could be a bit more grateful for his efforts. He's trying to help us.'

Redfern snorted at this assertion, but chose to make no further derisory comments.

'So, tell me what the Lincolnshire force has been doing,' Casey invited Moon. 'Have they any person they're particularly interested in?'

'Dylan Harper, for one, seeing as he's being as unhelpful as he can be. They were certainly long enough questioning him.'

'Bloody cops!' Foxy was back to his previous belligerent form, clearly unable to contain his prejudices even when it was in his best interests to do so. 'They only confiscated all our cannabis plants, not just the ones outside, but the ones in the loft as well. What are we supposed to do for bread now? Try to help yourself and be self-supporting and the cops are down on you like a ton of bricks.'

That there were other cannabis plants growing on the smallholding was news to Casey.

'You had cannabis growing in the loft?' How very enterprising, he thought, wondering which of the raggle-taggle band had thought of it and found the energy to get it under way.

'Yeah. It was Kris's idea,' Foxy told him, surprisingly not trying to take the credit for this unsuspected entrepreneurial spirit. 'It cost, mind, but we bypassed the electricity to light the plants to lessen the outlay. We grew them in a hydroponic solution – a nutrient solution for the roots which accelerates growth,' Foxy explained before he scowled. 'When I think of all the work and debt to get it up and running, I could kill someone.'

'Indeed,' was Casey's comment. 'And did you?'

'No, I didn't. Maybe you ought to look closer to home for your killer, instead of levelling accusations at me.'

'It wasn't an accusation, Mr Redfern, merely a question.' Casey, who considered cannabis a dangerous gateway drug to worse drugs – look what a scrambled mess it had made of his father's mind and memory – had little sympathy for their losses. Though he was more than surprised that the commune had got a hydroponic system up, running and producing a profit. He was surprised also that Catt hadn't mentioned it, but perhaps with two murders his police contact hadn't thought the drugs growing in the loft worth telling him about. But growing cannabis under such conditions indicated a certain professionalism at work; the plants required a lot of care and attention, particularly given the attendant fire risk and the fact that the plants required darkness as well as light to grow. It was a level of care that Casey couldn't envisage any of the commune members capable of. Yet one of them, at least, must have found previously unsuspected inner resources after Callender's death to keep the production up and running. Especially judging by the commune's new and expensive possessions, which he now took for granted hadn't been purchased with money from a lottery win at all.

'Is there any indication that they're soon to make an arrest for the two murders?' he asked Moon. ThomCatt hadn't seemed to think this was likely in the near future, but it didn't hurt to ask one of those in the centre of the whirlwind.

'Who's to say? They play their cards close to their chest, as I told you, and have kept us in the dark as to what they're thinking.'

Casey wasn't surprised. It was the police way to keep suspects guessing. Anxiety often made people reveal more than was wise. 'I suppose, as well as all being charged with growing cannabis with intent to supply, you're also being charged with bypassing the electric meter and stealing electricity?' Catt had confided this titbit, but Casey thought he might as well get it from the horses' mouths. He and Catt had both assumed this electricity bypass was simply their normal behaviour rather than done in order to lessen the massive use of electricity that hydroponic growth of cannabis required.

'Such a shame they found the plants in the loft,' Moon said wistfully. 'They were doing well, really lush. Our second crop was nearly ready for harvesting, too. We'll miss the money it'd have brought in.'

If this was a subtle hint to Casey, he chose to ignore it. He'd bailed his parents out often enough in the past, but this was one occasion when they'd have to fund their own irresponsible lifestyle. It was enough that he was attempting to investigate who was responsible for the killings. Moon really was incorrigible, he thought. Why couldn't she and the rest of the commune members get jobs like normal human beings? There were plenty of women of Moon's age still working and contributing to society. But instead of getting jobs, the whole pack of them were on assorted benefits. It made him cross. They certainly hadn't registered the smallholding as a business with all the tax implications that would bring. Even though they were all able-bodied enough to work, they much preferred the government to pay *them* rather than the other way about. A bit of decent, honest labour might do them the world of good.

Casey left soon after without seeing the elusive Dylan Harper. He felt dispirited in mind and body. But then this feeling was the inevitable result of a visit to the commune. It was the reason he had always chosen to visit but rarely.

As Moon locked the gate behind him, Casey told her to keep her eyes and ears open, said goodnight and climbed back into his car. He decided to return to the office and put in an hour on the paperwork on the Gus Oliver killing before he went home. He was reflective as he drove away, disturbed by his thoughts on the efficient cannabis factory in the commune's loft. His parents would never have got that up and running on their own, that was for sure. So far, his parents had never, whatever other culpable acts they might have gone in for, done anything of such a seriously criminal nature that the police had

needed to check deeply into their lives or backgrounds.
Petty offences, mostly drug-related, were the sum total
of their criminality. Plus a bit of thieving in his father's
misspent youth.

But now, with two dead bodies found on their smallholding, Casey couldn't believe he would be able to remain
anonymous for much longer. Surely someone would soon
sniff out his existence? Worriedly, he drove on into the dark
Fens night.

Once in his office, he pulled a pile of statements on their
official investigation towards him and began to read. His
concentration on this task was so great that he didn't hear
Catt enter.

'Got some news.' Catt told Casey's bent head.

Casey dragged his gaze from the latest statement and
stared at Catt, surprised to find him in the station so late
rather than out with the latest girlfriend. 'Who from? This
from your policeman friend or from one of your old
friends?'

'My friend in the Lincolnshire force was unavailable
when I rang. In a powwow in the incident room probably. No, this info was from another of my contacts who
lives close to the commune. I hadn't been able to get hold
of him before as he's been out of the country for a few
days. Seems the late DaisyMay had been seen in one of
the local pubs several times with Kris Callender. They
chose a pub that wasn't the commune members' usual
haunt, but one a bit out of the way. Perfect for a clan-
destine assignation.'

'Might mean something or nothing. You said they were
seen together more than once?'

Catt nodded. 'And by someone who knew them both by
sight and has no axe to grind.'

'Could just be a coincidence. Did your contact happen
to notice how they behaved towards one another?'

'He said they seemed very touchy-feely. But that also
might mean something or nothing, seeing as they're all so
into love and peace, man, at the commune, they're probably

all touchy-feely. Maybe they were having an affair and maybe they weren't. But if the former is the case, it gives our grieving widower an excellent motive for murdering DaisyMay. An excellent motive, too, for offing Callender. The only difficulty there is why he killed them two months apart. Unless, like young Madonna, she was up the duff by the dear departed.'

'Mmm. If Harper's blood was up for that reason, I'd have thought he'd kill them both at the same time. Still. Well done, ThomCatt. It gives us another possibility to look into.' He paused. 'I've got some news as well.' He told Catt about the commune growing cannabis in the loft.

Catt whistled. 'Enterprising. Wouldn't have thought they were up to it.'

'My sentiments exactly. From what Foxy Redfern said, it would seem the late Mr Callender was the driving force behind it.'

'He seems to have been the driving force behind a lot of things. I'm surprised one of them killed him in that case. Why kill the laying goose?'

'For reasons other than their profitable drug business if it was one of the commune who killed him. Or, if it was an outsider, which I still think unlikely, it seems he could have been killed because he unwisely tried to cheat the wrong people. But as we don't know anything for sure, that's just another question to add to the growing pile. I hope we're able to begin answering some of them soon.' Casey stood up. 'That's it for tonight. I'm taking in little or nothing. And tomorrow's another day.'

'Probably bringing more questions with it, too.'

The next morning dawned bright and clear. Casey woke before the alarm went and he turned it off so as not to wake Rachel. The orchestra in which she was a violinist had been rehearsing late the previous night and she had been dog tired when she returned home. Rachel's unsocial hours were something he was grateful for – they mirrored his own. The hours were often the main reason for police couples splitting up. But given her own hours, Rachel would never be able to throw his in his face as so many other wives and partners did.

He quickly showered and pulled underwear from the drawer, a clean shirt from the wardrobe and a fresh suit. He'd get dressed downstairs so as not to disturb her.

Later, dressed and sipping coffee at the kitchen table, he ruminated on the two cases, reflecting that the unofficial one seemed to be making more progress, mostly no thanks to him, than his official investigation. Not for the first time, he thanked God for Thomas Catt's ill-assorted contacts; but for them he would never have known about the touchy-feely meetings between DaisyMay and Callender.

And this evening they were to interview Carole Brown, the third unalibied member of Gus Oliver's harem. Maybe, if she or Max Fallon, her partner, were guilty of murder, they'd give themselves away, thereby providing answers on their official investigation.

On this optimistic note, Casey finished the last of his coffee, shrugged into his jacket and let himself out of the house.

More statements awaited his attention when Casey arrived at his office. He was ploughing his way through them when Catt popped his head around the door several hours later.

'Anything of interest?' He gestured at the pile of statements as he entered.

'Not so you'd notice,' Casey replied. He dropped the statement he had been reading back on the pile and straightened up. 'Things are moving very slowly on this case,' he complained. 'Let's hope this evening's interview shakes something loose. Remind me what we know about this Ms Brown and her live-in partner.'

Catt pulled the chair from in front of Casey's desk, turned it so the back was towards Casey and dropped in to it, crossing his arms on the top bar. 'Her partner, Max Fallon, is a bit of a wide boy. Owns several nightclubs in the area, including the one here in town. On the criminal fringe with ambitions. He's done time for assault. As for Carole Brown, she seemed a bit of a slut to me. Surprisingly, she's nothing

like Oliver's other lady loves, all of whom are very feminine and rather less obvious. Guess Ms Brown must have
been Oliver's bit of rough.'

'Interesting that her partner brings a criminal element,
a violent element to the case, especially given the bloody
mode of Oliver's death. Cutting off his penis might be
just Fallon's mode of operation. It would certainly act as
a deterrent to anyone else hoping to step into Oliver's
shoes.'

'Or his trousers.'

'Or his trousers. It's got more than a touch of the gang-
ster's revenge about it.'

'Mmm,' Catt murmured. 'That's what I thought. And from
what I've learned of Fallon, he's not the type to turn a blind
eye if his partner's been playing away. I don't know whether
he found out about his girlfriend's fling with Gus Oliver,
but I forgot to tell you that she was sporting a spectacular
black eye when I questioned her.'

'Should make for an intriguing interview. I wonder how
she'll say she came by it.'

'The usual walked into a door scenario, probably.'

Casey glanced at his watch, surprised to see that it was
already one o'clock. 'Fancy lunch at the Lamb?' he asked
Catt. 'My treat.'

'Sounds good, especially the bit about you paying.'

'Let's just say it's my thank you for services rendered
on the commune case.'

The Lamb was but a short drive away. Casey pulled up
and parked in the car park. Practically full, the number of
cars shouted that summer had arrived. After all the chilly,
grey days, July had finally recalled it was meant to be warm
and had come out in a blaze of sunny glory.

The pub was their usual haunt when the canteen fare at
the station palled. An old coaching inn, it was situated on
the banks of the river and had pleasant gardens, just perfect
to sit out on such a fine day.

'Just a salad for me, please,' Casey told the barmaid.
'Chicken, I think.' He turned to Catt. 'Made your mind up,
ThomCatt?'

Catt nodded. 'I'll have the chicken casserole, please, my darling.'

Casey sighed at the evidence that he hadn't managed to break his sergeant of being over-familiar, took their food tickets and went and got the drinks while Catt found an unoccupied table outside.

'This is the life,' Catt remarked as Casey arrived with the drinks.

'Mmm,' Casey agreed as he sat down. 'Enjoy it while you can. We can't stay long. Duty will call all too soon.'

'Don't go and spoil it,' Catt teased. 'With two investigations on the go, I reckon we've earned a bit of R and R.'

'Some might say we've earned nothing until the cases are wrapped up and the murderers in the cells.'

Catt just shrugged at this and took a long drink from his lager. 'Fallon and his girlfriend seem a rum pair,' he observed. 'I'll be interested to get your take on them. Wonder why she stays with him if he beats her up.'

'Unfathomable are the ways of women.'

Catt nodded. 'I suppose the money's a draw. Doubtless it helps to ease the pain. And with a string of nightclubs, he can't be short of a few bob. Maybe enough to pay a hit man to do his dirty work for him.'

'Mmm. As you say, he sounds something of a fly-boy, our Fallon. His record marks him out as a nasty piece of work.'

'So you reckon him for our killer?' Catt asked just as their food arrived.

Casey waited until the girl had served them and returned inside before he replied. 'Given his reputation and record, it seems a strong possibility.'

Catt pondered this for a second or two as he picked up his cutlery. 'Maybe it would be *too* easy.'

Casey smiled and started on his salad. 'Thought you were looking for the easy life, ThomCatt, taking your leisure in the sunshine?'

'Who? Me? No. I want to catch our killers, both here and up in Lincolnshire. Even if we'll never get the credit for solving those killings.'

'We've got to catch the murderers yet, before we can talk of taking credit,' Casey reminded him again. 'So eat up and let us at least make a stab – excuse the pun – at catching the killer here.'

Thirteen

They were lucky that evening and managed to interview Carole Brown alone as her partner had been delayed; Casey hoped she might be more forthcoming without Fallon's intimidating presence.

The pair, like the other couples they had already interviewed, lived in some style. Theirs was an apartment like the Garretts', but all similarity ended at the name. Part of an old warehouse block, the interior was very spacious. But the space had been filled with upmarket tat of high expense and dubious taste. No scheme of colour or style had been selected to provide harmony; the place was a mishmash of whatever had taken their fancy and they seemed to fancy the garish above all.

Casey didn't wait for an invitation, but sank into a bright orange plastic chair. Catt selected another in deep purple while Casey began the questioning.

'I understand you were at home alone all evening last Friday?'

Carole Brown threw herself down on a lime green settee without a response. She seemed sullen and inclined to be tetchy when the questioning began, constantly fingering her ripe black eye and scowling. As Casey had said, she was yet another one who had claimed to be home all evening, with no one to back up her tale, on the night Oliver was murdered.

'And what about your boyfriend, Mr Fallon? Was he home all evening?' Casey questioned.

'Max? Not likely. He was out, wheeling and dealing, as usual. I already told *him* that.' She jerked her head in Catt's direction.

'Bit of a Del Boy, is he, your partner?' Catt asked as he raised his head from his notebook.

'Thinks he is, more like.'

Carole Brown certainly seemed to be nursing a grievance against her partner; easy to understand given the shiner. 'Mr Fallon has a conviction for assault and seems to mix with questionable acquaintances,' Casey remarked. 'Did he give you that black eye?'

'Certainly not. The wind blew the front door back in my face.' She stared at them as if expecting them not to believe her. 'He's a lamb is my Maxie. He'd never hit a woman.' Even her words held a certain cynicism as if she found amusement in saying them. Perhaps she even believed them, though given her streetwise appearance, it seemed unlikely. Maybe it was her pride talking.

'While Mr Fallon's not here, perhaps you could tell us something about your relationship with the late Mr Oliver?'

Carole Brown sneered. 'What's this, Discretion Is Us? And to call it a relationship is stretching it a bit far. We met for sex, that's about as far as any relationship went. He bought me a few trinkets which I had to hock in case Max found them and started asking questions.' Her thin lips tightened. 'It's just as well the bastard's dead or I'd have killed him myself.'

'Why's that?' Casey asked.

'Bastard gave me the clap, that's why. He never used condoms. Complained they were uncomfortable and took away from the sensations. It wouldn't have mattered too much, only before I knew I had it, I'd passed it on to Max.' Involuntarily, she touched her black eye, giving the lie to her tale of the wind-blown front door. At Catt's grin, she pulled a face and admitted the truth.

'All right. I lied. I got this when Max started getting symptoms and had them checked out. He slapped me around till he learned the name of the culprit who'd given me the disease.'

Casey's gaze met Catt's as the significance of this sank in: Fallon, prone to violence and with a conviction for assault, would be unlikely to take kindly to a man who had not only persuaded his girlfriend to be unfaithful, but who had also infected them both with gonorrhoea. Had they found Oliver's killer so soon?

The front door slammed and a sour-faced Max Fallon entered the room. He was tall with hair that was styled to within an inch of its life; he had that much in common with Catt, but that was where the similarity ended. He wore a flashy suit of a light mauve with a white stripe. He loosened his tie and unbuttoned his collar as he came towards them. He selected a chair and sat back, seemingly at his ease, before he directed a grey-eyed and challenging stare at the two policemen. It seemed he had no difficulty in recognizing their profession, for he said sharply, 'Cops? What are you doing here? My club licenses are already renewed.'

'We're not here about your licenses, Mr Fallon,' Casey said. He began to introduce himself and Catt, but Fallon waived away his words.

'No need for introductions, gentlemen. It's my belief that when you've met one cop you've met 'em all.' He sat forward and demanded, 'So, what's she told you? Did the dirty bitch tell you she gave me the clap?' It was clear from his manner than Fallon had been drinking a little too unwisely. If he hadn't been he would surely had kept that gem of a motive to himself.

'Indeed she did, Mr Fallon,' Casey replied. 'She also told us who gave it to her. A man who has since died very violently. Did you perhaps decide to take revenge on Mr Oliver?'

'I might have done if I'd managed to catch up with him,' was the candid reply. He removed his tie, by the simple expedient of pulling the loosened garment over his head before he flung it in the corner. 'But this is one thing you can't pin on me. I was at my club till the early hours on Friday night. Ask any of my staff there.'

'Oh, I will, Mr Fallon,' said Casey, though he thought asking Fallon's staff such a question was likely to prove singularly unproductive. Given Fallon's tendency to violence it was unlikely any of his staff would be so foolhardy as to contradict him. Fallon could easily have slipped out and laid in wait near Oliver's house for him to emerge. A knife would be an excellent incentive to get him to the dark edge of the rubbish-strewn alley. It would have been the work of moments to stab Oliver in the groin. Cutting off the victim's penis and stuffing it in his mouth, would – if the knife was sharp and Casey doubted that Max Fallon would carry anything but a slick and sharpened blade – have taken little longer.

It certainly seemed the sort of crime that had Fallon's name all over it: most criminals progressed up the ladder of villainy and violence over time, so, given the provocation of a sexually transmitted disease and having been thoroughly cuckolded, such a leap up the ranks of the criminal fraternity didn't seem unlikely.

The only difficulty with this was Dr Merriman's emphatic insistence that Oliver's body had been moved after death. If Fallon had lain in wait for Oliver outside the latter's home, he could, of course, have bundled him into a car, but the argument against this was that unless it was a stolen vehicle, which he thought unlikely in Fallon's case, he wouldn't want Oliver's blood on his seat covers. And if he had walked his victim to the alleyway at knifepoint and killed him there, the body wouldn't provide evidence of its transport from somewhere else. It was a conundrum, the answer to which evaded Casey. But one thing he could do was to get Catt to look again through the CCTC footage. They'd need to check what car Fallon drove – this was something he preferred not to ask Fallon directly. CCTV was more likely to tell them the truth than either Fallon or his hired help.

'I'd like the names of the staff you claim can provide you with an alibi, Mr Fallon,' Casey told him in spite of the belief that getting these names would be a waste of time.

Fallon didn't demure. With an expression that tended to the smug, he reeled them off. Catt noted them down.

'We'll be paying a visit to your local club, sir,' he told Fallon. 'It was the one in King's Langley rather than one of your other establishments where you claim to have been?'

'That's right.' Fallon nodded. 'King's in the High Street. And not "claimed", but *was*. My staff will, I'm sure, be glad to assist you.' His still smug expression foretold the opposite.

'We'll be in touch, sir,' Casey murmured as they headed for the door.

'Please do, Chief Inspector. I always aim to help the police.'

'He's certainly done that a few times,' was Catt's comment once they were on the other side of the front door. 'Let's hope he's not guilty of *this* crime because alibied up as he is, we're unlikely to prove it. He'll have primed his staff with the answers he wants.'

'Don't I know it. Still, the CCTV might, with luck, contradict him and them. We'll question his staff this evening, anyway. Maybe one of the regular customers will spill any beans to be had.'

'Only the more idiotic of them would do so, given Fallon's tendency for violence.'

'We must hope we hit on an idiot, then, as it seems the only way we're likely to get some straight answers. Unless he proves to be the idiot and we find his car captured by the CCTV cameras heading towards Oliver's home. I want you to check it out as soon as possible.'

Catt nodded. And with thoughts of idiots to comfort them, they headed back to the station.

Max Fallon's nightclub was the usual combination of loud strobe lighting and even louder music – if such it could be called. Its garish colours and furniture bore a marked similarity to those of his apartment. Perhaps he had bought a job lot at a knock-down price.

But, as Fallon claimed in his advertisements, his club attracted celebrities; according to the barman they had two weather girls as regulars. He had seemed quite proud of the fact that the club could boast such Z-listers amongst their clientele. It was comforting to Casey to discover that Fallon wasn't as high up the totem pole as he would have liked them to believe. People of influence were one of the banes of a copper's life, so it was good to learn that the nightclub owner's was only likely to be as high as that of his 'celebrity' clients.

The barman and the rest of the staff were quick to confirm what Fallon had told them – that he hadn't left the club till around four on Saturday morning, at which time Gus Oliver's body must already have begun to cool. Presumably, as Casey had anticipated, Fallon had rung his staff after he and Catt had left the apartment and primed them with what they were to say. But at least, during their earlier scout around the car park, they had spotted what had seemed likely to be Fallon's car and had rung in for confirmation of ownership.

Max Fallon, perhaps in order to live up to his would-be reputation as a favourite of celebrities, drove a silver Porsche with a personalized registration.

'At least it should be easy to spot on the CCTV tapes,' was Catt's comment.

The nightclub visit hadn't been the waste of time that Casey had expected. But if the CCTV footage failed to come up trumps they would, in the lack of any other evidence to connect Fallon to the crime, have to pursue their inquiries elsewhere.

Once they had left King's nightclub and returned to the station car park, they headed their separate ways – Catt off on a 'hot' date and Casey home to Rachel.

She'd made a casserole, she told him when he arrived home, rather to his surprise, after he'd kissed her hello. In her lack of domesticity, he had often thought that Rachel would fit right in with Moon, Star and the commune lifestyle, which was why he usually made sure to have a hot meal in the police canteen. She had a touch of the Bohemian about her. Perhaps it was because she led such a gypsy existence with her music and the orchestra. However, grateful for the hot meal to quieten the hunger pangs, he spooned out a generous portion of the casserole and returned to the living room with his steaming plate.

'So how are your two investigations progressing?' Rachel

asked from the depths of the settee, where she lay stretched out like a cat.

'My murders are going as well as can be expected,' he told her solemnly, 'which is pretty poorly.'

'That bad, huh?'

'That bad. We seem to be getting nowhere with our official inquiry, at least.' He paused. 'Well, I suppose that's not strictly true. There are a number of possibilities with that one. As to the murders at the commune, it seems the late DaisyMay might well have been a tad over friendly with Kris Callender.'

'What? They were having an affair, you mean?'

Casey waited till he had swallowed another mouthful of casserole before he replied. 'It's a possibility, seeing as those at the commune are so into making love and not war – though, according to Moon, war's been breaking out all over lately. Anyway, the possibility that DaisyMay and Callender were sleeping together means it might not be her husband's baby she was carrying.'

'Interesting.'

'I thought so. Which is why I suggested that Catt put the idea of blood or DNA tests to his tame policeman so he could pass the idea on to his boss. DNA would be the clincher; it's the only way we'll find out just whose baby DaisyMay was carrying. Though contradictory to that theory, I have to wonder from Dylan's protective behaviour towards her whether he suspected a thing. At least, according to Moon, Catt's policeman friend has managed to persuade his superiors that DNA tests are necessary. It could save a lot of time and suspicions.'

'Only if Dylan, DaisyMay's partner, knew she was carrying another man's child, and you said there's no evidence for that.'

'True. In fact, given his solicitous behaviour right up to her death, all the evidence points the other way.' Casey finished his meal and put the bowl on the table. 'That was delicious. I was ready for it.

'Without the DNA evidence, there's apparently little else to point to the guilty party,' Casey said as he leant back and rubbed his tired eyes. 'Though seeing as the dogs didn't start to bark anywhere around the time DaisyMay must have been killed, the commune's marked preference for a guilty outsider is unlikely to hold water. It seems her murderer has to be one of the commune members. As to Kris Callender's murder, the perpetrator is anyone's guess. Not only did it happen weeks ago, but he seems to have spent his time putting everyone's backs up, so the field's wide open.

'It's surprising really that we haven't got a chief suspect, given what a slapdash, drugged-up lot they are in that commune. You'd have expected the murderer or murderers – though I can't believe there are two of them in such a small community – to be careless about leaving clues to their identity behind. But whoever killed the pair was smart enough not to contaminate the scene of DaisyMay's murder. It's too late, of course, to check out any such traces from Kris Callender's murder as he's been in the ground for around two months if not longer – they're not terribly precise on dates at the commune.' He paused. 'By the way, I meant to ask you – how did your rehearsal go?'

'I thought it went well, but Mr Baton Man clearly didn't agree with me. He threw a massive hissy fit and made us work later that anticipated. Lucky I put the casserole in the slow cooker before I went out.' She sat up straighter. 'But I don't want to talk about him. I have enough of him all day without allowing him to dominate my free time as well. In fact –' she swung herself off the settee in one lithe movement – 'I'm for bed.' She reached the door and gave him a come hither look. 'What about you?'

Casey needed no second invitation.

It was raining when Casey got up the next morning; a veritable downpour. Summer hadn't lasted long in spite of the weathermen's optimistic predictions. He could hear the rain hammering against the window as he got dressed.

He made coffee and brought both cups upstairs. It was Rachel's day off and Casey asked her what she was going to do with it.

'I thought I might try some more retail therapy and spend some of your hard-earned money.'

'Just as well one of us is a good earner,' Casey smiled. As an orchestral musician, Rachel didn't earn good money; for her the labour was for love rather than filthy lucre. 'I certainly never seem to get time for shopping.'

'All the more for me, then.'

Casey finished his coffee, kissed Rachel goodbye and ran through the downpour to his car.

As the questioning of the staff and trickle of early customers at Max Fallon's' nightclub had yielded little to go on, Casey knew they would have to dig deeper. It was a shame they still had no results, Casey mused, as he stared down at the latest reports that had come in. He had to outline the progress on the case to Superintendent Brown-Smith later. Unless Catt's re-watching of the CCTV tapes bore fruit he didn't know what he could tell him, though he supposed he should be grateful that, unlike in his previous case, the victims weren't Asian. Brown-Smith was so politically correct he always preferred his suspected criminals to be white; it confirmed his prejudices. And as he remembered his last telephone conversation with Moon, Casey could only imagine how hot his superintendent's prejudice would run if they were officially investigating the deaths at the commune. He supposed he should be grateful for small mercies.

Moon had told him the murders had, in their wake, brought an atmosphere you could cut with a knife. Several of the commune had taken to barring their bedroom doors at night. And not just the commune women: Scott 'Mackenzie' Johnson and Randy Matthews had, by Moon's account, taken similar precautions.

'Willow Tree,' his mother had pleaded, 'hurry up and find the killer before the commune is destroyed. Star and me are too old to start over somewhere else.'

He had assured her he was trying. 'But it's a bit difficult attempting to solve a case as I'm doing, at one remove.' Especially when he was receiving so little help from the commune members themselves. He paused, not sure he really wanted an answer to the question he had felt forced to ask several times already, but he posed it anyway. 'How's Star bearing up?'

'He's all right. Nothing much affects him. Not now he's getting his normal ration of sleep, anyway. He's as laid-back as ever, but then he's never been one of life's worriers, though I was anxious he'd blurt something out to the cops.'

'He didn't though?' Casey broke in urgently. 'You said he hadn't.'

'No. But it was a close run thing. You know how out of it he can get. At such times he'll tell anybody anything. I had to sit beside him and keep pinching him when he was questioned.'

'Surely the police questioned him alone?'

Moon laughed. 'They tried to. But all they got was mono-syllables. In the end they admitted defeat and allowed me in to prompt him – not that they got much more sense out of him then – something I made sure of, as you can imagine, hon.'

The court case was scheduled for later that afternoon and Casey could only hope his father maintained this Sphinx-like silence. He'd be on tenterhooks till it was over. It wasn't even as if he could attend in case someone recognized him. He'd just have to rely on Moon's report afterwards – always assuming their brief managed to get bail for the pair . . .

Casey glanced at his watch and sighed. He still had a lot to do before he could set off for the Fens and the commune to see how the court case had gone and, now they'd had time to let the consequences sink in, how the murders had affected them all after they'd been questioned at the hands of a prosecutor.

Catt came into the office. 'I've worked my way through two of the CCTV tapes,' he told Casey. 'I'll try the rest when we get back.'

Casey nodded. Soon after, he and Catt were on their way to see the Merediths again.

So far, several of Oliver's lovers and their partners had

signally failed to provide alibis worthy of the name. And the Merediths were no better in this regard than the Garretts or Max Fallon and Carole Brown.

Once they were admitted to the Merediths' expensive detached home and seated in the living room, Casey became aware of a simmering atmosphere. Had Roger Meredith succeeded in getting the truth from his wife about her infidelity? Had she admitted it after their visit in response to her husband's probing? Or had he discovered it prior to Oliver's murder and concealed the knowledge, only now, after Casey and Catt's previous visit, letting his suspicions surface?

'I think it's safe to say, Mr and Mrs Meredith,' Casey began, 'that neither of you have an alibi for the night Mr Oliver was murdered.'

'No. That's true enough,' Meredith blithely confirmed. 'Though why you think we need alibis is beyond me. I barely knew the man and he was nothing more than a some-time acquaintance of my wife. Isn't that so, Amanda?'

Amanda gave a brief nod.

Casey stared at Meredith. Meredith stared back as if daring Casey to contradict him. But he got the strongest feeling that Roger Meredith *had* known that Gus Oliver was rather more than a 'sometime acquaintance' of Amanda's. He wondered if Oliver had also passed gonorrhoea on to her. It seemed a distinct possibility. Had she, in turn, passed it on to her husband? Or had she or one of the other harem members been the one to pass the disease on to Oliver? If Meredith hadn't been playing away himself, he, like Max Fallon, would know his wife had been unfaithful as soon as he had his symptoms checked out. No wonder, if so, that the atmosphere felt so tense. Such a betrayal would stick in the craw of anyone.

According to what the Merediths had told them so far, they had both been at home at the relevant times – Mrs Meredith watching television in the first-floor living room and her husband working in his study at the top of the house. Either could have sneaked out without the other being aware of it. It would, of course, have been taking a chance, but presumably they were each sufficiently familiar with the other's habits and routines and would know when the other was settled for several hours.

Amanda Meredith was more voluptuous than either Carole Brown or Sarah Garrett. She also struck Casey as, beneath her frilly femininity, being tougher than either of the other two women.

Roger Meredith was rangy and lean and looked to keep himself very fit. He was good-looking in a sharp-faced way and dressed expensively and well. It was clear he was a man with more than his share of pride. How must he and the other harem husbands/boyfriends have felt when, in Fallon's case, and if in that of the other men they had discovered their partners' infidelity? Casey guessed Meredith, for one, wouldn't sit back and take it. He also guessed he would find it hard, if not impossible, to forgive. He would want revenge on someone. Though whether that someone was his wife or Gus Oliver was something they had still to discover.

'Are you sure that neither of you went out that evening?' he asked.

Meredith answered with a sharpness that equalled his angular features. 'I told you, we were both at home all evening.'

Casey thought it would be worth questioning the neighbours again. He'd do that in any case, as part of the normal house-to-house routine. But this time, to judge from the shiftiness of Roger Meredith's gaze, he thought he might just get something useful. Maybe there was a lonely old woman in their street who had nothing better to do with her time than watch the neighbours' comings and goings.

But, for now, it was clear they would get nothing more out of the pair but pleas of innocence, which, for all Casey knew, might even be true.

Back in the car on the way to the station, he and Catt discussed the case.

'Gus Oliver really set the cat among the pigeons with these three couples, didn't he?' Catt commented. 'Do you think Oliver knew he'd caught the clap? And was he impervious to who he passed it on to?'

'God knows. But symptoms of STDs show up far quicker in men than women, so it's a possibility he knew and carried on regardless.'

'If so, it seems possible one of the six thought he deserved to die. It's like those cases of men – it's usually men – who have unprotected sex knowing they have the HIV virus.'

Casey went down to second gear as he approached the red traffic light at the corner. He changed the subject and told Catt, 'I'm going to the commune tonight. I want to hear from the horses' mouths how the court case against them went. I think I'll have a chance of getting more out of Moon if I'm there in body rather than just a voice over the telephone.'

'Well, just be careful. And check around the lanes yourself before you approach the commune. It's possible the Boston cops have been trying to lull them into a false sense of security by removing their presence, only to take up a watching brief on the place again. The last thing you want is to risk them becoming aware of the association. It wouldn't do your promotion prospects much good if it became known. You might even need your Get out of Jail Free card.'

'Remind me to take it out of the Monopoly set before I go.' Casey gave a wry smile as he moved the gear stick into first and pulled away from the lights.

Superintendent Brown-Smith was in a sour mood when Casey went to see him to report on their progress on Gus Oliver's murder. His mood wasn't improved by the lack of results on the case.

'You'll have to do better than this, Casey,' Brown-Smith told him when Casey had outlined what was happening. 'It's the thin end of the widget.' The superintendent had a habit of mangling his metaphors and vocabulary, especially when agitated. 'You have enough suspects. What about this Fallon type? He sounds a likely prospect. I want you to look deeper into his motions.'

'We're already doing that, sir,' Casey replied, understanding his boss's intended meaning, and trying to expunge from his mind the bizarre picture the superintendent had unintentionally conjured up. 'Catt's looking through the CCTV footage again to see if he can spot Fallon's car anywhere close to the alley where the body was found.' Indeed, anywhere at all at the relevant times, Casey thought, seeing as Fallon had been emphatic that he'd left the night-club in the early hours of Saturday morning.

'He won't see it if the man left his club with murder in mind. He sounds to me to be smart enough to take steps to avoid incriminating himself.'

Casey swallowed an involuntary sigh at this self-evident truth.

'You'll need to check the footage for the cars of his staff as well. Likely he borrowed a vehicle from one of them.'

'Yes, sir. I'll get Catt or one of the others to do that as well.' He already had that in hand, but it was as well to humour Brown-Smith by letting him think he was the only one with the good ideas.

The superintendent let him go soon after.

Catt was still checking out the CCTV footage when Casey set off for the Fens. He couldn't help but wonder what he'd find at the smallholding now the atmosphere of fear and suspicion had had time to breed.

Fourteen

As Casey got nearer to the smallholding, in the distance he could see Boston Stump dominating the grey skyline. This was the name given to the tower of St Botolph's Church and was a misnomer since the tower, to Casey's knowledge, soared not far off 300 feet and could be seen for thirty miles around. Apart from the misnamed tower, the church was well known for its abundance of bizarre medieval carvings in wood and stone: a bear playing an organ; a man lassoing a lion; a fox in a bishop's cope taking a jug of water from a baboon. Moon had told him about them and he had gone to see them himself on an earlier visit.

But now was not the time for musing on bizarre carvings, he told himself as he approached the smallholding and braced himself for an unfriendly welcome.

The brand new 4 x 4 had vanished from the smallholding's yard, Casey immediately noticed as he pulled up. Had some of them gone for a joyride after the court case and an unexpectedly good result? he wondered as Moon opened the gate and let him in. He shrugged and thought no more about it apart from going in for a brief headcount as he entered the living room. As expected, the elusive Dylan Harper was still conspicuous by his absence; probably he was once more secreted in his bedroom away from those he presumably suspected of murdering DaisyMay.

His headcount revealed that Scott 'Mackenzie' Johnson and his lover, Randy Matthews, were not amongst the motley crew sprawled about the untidy living room. They had previously been a silent but visible presence, sitting close together and seemingly with eyes only for each other. Casey questioned Moon and soon learned that, unlike the rest, Randy and Scott had decided to remove themselves from the area of suspicion.

'They've done a bunk? And taken the four by four?'

Moon gave a glum nod.

The taking of the new car clearly rankled: was Moon getting a liking for the pleasures of property ownership in her middle years?

'Randy must have persuaded Scott the police would be on their case, you lot being so against their kind.'

Casey smothered an amused smile. She wouldn't say that if she knew Superintendent Brown-Smith. It was his own kind he had a down on. He was almost as keen on homosexuals as he was on ethnics; he even wore a ribbon in his lapel on Gay Pride days, so determined was he to suck up to minorities. Anyway, doubtless DI Boxham would have circulated the details of the car as Casey presumed the pair had failed to show up at court.

Moon confirmed it.

'Any idea where they've gone?' he questioned the room generally. But no one knew the pair's whereabouts. Or, if they did, they weren't saying. Unsurprisingly, the commune, in spite of the festering suspicions, seemed to have closed ranks even against Casey, who was doing his best to help them.

'Dare I presume that you've reported their disappearance to the police?' Casey asked.

'Hey man,' Foxy Redfern put in, 'we just have, right?'

Casey breathed in on a sigh and told him, 'You know very well that I'm investigating unofficially and can't report my findings to the Lincolnshire police. You'll have to do it. It'll look better if it seems you're trying to help them.' As opposed to hindering them, which was what they seemed determined to do to him. He was surprised Boxham hadn't called in to question them, but when he asked about this he learned the police had so far failed to put in an appearance. But they might yet do so, he realized, so he told them he was moving his car to the rear as a precaution and went out.

When he returned to the living room, he asked, 'So when did you notice they'd gone?'

'Latish this morning,' Moon told him. 'When they hadn't stirred from their room for our court appearance I went and checked on them. All their stuff had gone. They'd even taken all our scented candles.' Moon sounded even more put out at this than she had at the loss of the 4 x 4.

'Well, they did buy them,' Kali put in. 'Why shouldn't they take them?'

Moon, in spite of her firm belief that property was theft and that everything in the commune belonged to them all, clearly excluded the purchasers of the candles in her Utopian vision. But, equally clearly, she had no answer to Kali's pert observation.

'Would they have gone on the road?' Casey asked. 'Joined a bunch of travellers, perhaps?'

Moon scoffed. 'Not those two. Very particular, they were. Forever complaining about what they called our slovenly habits. They'll have found some comfortable place to nest in.'

'Real pair of queens, those two,' Foxy put in from the sofa where he had again taken up a sprawling residence. 'Our ways weren't good enough for them. Just as well they've gone. I've longed to boot them out for some time. Can't stand fairies, man. The way they used to keep their own company as if the rest of us weren't good enough for them stuck in my craw.'

Yet more evidence of their brotherly love, Casey thought as he nodded. In spite of his misgivings about the furnishings, he propped himself on the arm of one of the moth-eaten settees, determined to get something more in the way of information from them than he'd so far gained.

'You must know something,' he insisted, 'living cheek-by-jowl as you do. Come on, Moon.' He turned to his mother. 'Even if it's true that you don't know where our errant pair took themselves off to, you must have some idea as to who killed DaisyMay and Callender.' It was for certain, beyond a few unsubstantiated theories, that *he* didn't.

'You're all living in suspicion of one another. Surely it's better to get such suspicions out in the open?'

Moon didn't look too sure of this, so he mentioned that DaisyMay and Callender had been seen together in a local pub being very touchy-feely.

'Means nothing,' Moon told him. 'That's how we are. We love one another, man.'

Having just listened to Foxy Redfern's tirade of hate against the missing pair, Casey dredged up a faint smile at this.

'DaisyMay hadn't been feeling too well, what with her pregnancy. I imagine Kris had taken her out to cheer her up. It's what we do, hon: support one another.'

Only if they're as pretty as DaisyMay had been, in Callender's case, was Casey's immediate thought. He'd never noticed the man being touchy-feely or loving to anyone else, including his wife.

'Surely it was up to Dylan to offer solace and cider, rather than Kris Callender?' Casey remarked.

'We're family,' Moon insisted. 'We're not exclusive to our regular partners when someone else is in pain. Love, hon, is what it's all about.'

From what she had told him over the phone, the other women in the commune – who had taken to locking their bedroom doors at night – clearly didn't embrace this sentiment. Or, if they once had, they did so no longer.

Neither, it appeared, did Scott or Randy or their official detractor, Foxy.

But, if they suspected one another of murder, none of them was inclined just yet to grass to the cops, even one such as Casey. That much was clear. So after enquiring about the court case and getting mumbled responses, Casey heaved himself from the arm of the settee and left them to their mutual suspicions; maybe, given sufficient time, their suspicion and fear would overcome the brotherly love.

Swamped with possibilities on two murder investigations, Casey felt he needed a break. Rachel was playing in the orchestra in a local venue, so that evening, after visiting the commune and driving back to King's Langley, he took himself off to the local theatre. He arrived just on the interval when everyone was piling out to the bars to get their alcohol intake.

Casey joined the crowd. He was surprised to see Roger Meredith in the crush; he wouldn't have thought the rugby-playing Meredith inclined toward the arts. He was in deep conversation with another man at the corner of the bar. Casey edged closer to try to overhear what they were saying, but all it turned out to be was one of those rugger buggers' conversations about the merits of various wing-halves. He turned away before he was seen and, moving to the other end of the bar, he finally managed to attract the barman's attention and order a tonic water. Casey, unlike Catt, made it a point to never drink and drive.

The bell for the end of the interval rang soon after and he was carried along by the crowd back to the auditorium. He found his seat, and prepared to enjoy the orchestra's rendition of Brahms, but he found himself nodding off barely halfway through the piece and shrugged himself awake. It wouldn't do for Rachel to spot his drooping head. Even though she was unlikely to see him in the dim theatre, Casey sat up straighter and concentrated. He smiled at Rachel's serious face above her violin, her concentration fierce on her music; she made it a point to ignore the conductor as much as possible, as she found him overbearing.

Casey, as he watched her, found himself relaxing and getting into the music. The orchestra was good and the audience was appreciative in their applause as the concert drew to a close.

Casey fought his way against the human tide to the stage and caught up with Rachel before she disappeared into the wings.

'Why didn't you say you were coming?' Rachel asked. 'I'd have got you a front row seat.'

And catch me snoozing? Casey thought. 'I didn't know I'd be able to make it,' he excused himself. 'You were good. I enjoyed it. And knowing how hungry you always are after a concert, I thought I'd take you for a meal.'

'Great. Just give me time to get changed and I'm all yours.'

She disappeared into the wings and Casey waited. She was soon back, carrying her cased violin and the black dress she had performed in. 'Where are we going?' she asked as they left the theatre and made for the car.

'A little place Catt told me about,' he told her. 'New restaurant. Just opened.' Catt knew all the best haunts in the surrounding area; given his multiplicity of girlfriends, such knowledge was essential to his love life, or so he believed.

Not long after, they were seated at a table for two at a small Italian restaurant that exuded intimacy. Romantic Italian ballads wafted their love themes around the room followed by attentive waiters. They ordered spaghetti and Chianti. It wasn't long before Rachel asked him about his parents and their dilemma.

Casey shrugged, poured Rachel more wine and wound some more spaghetti around his fork. 'Nothing much to tell, beyond the fact their suspicions of one another seem to be growing. Oh, and two of commune have cleared out, bag and baggage.'

'Really? Who?'

'Funnily enough, it's the two I had least reason to suspect of murder. The two homosexuals, Randy and Scott.'

Rachel laughed. 'Why didn't you suspect them, Will? Because they're queer? You should play in the orchestra and see just how queer men can nurse grudges. Some of them have come to blows over accusations of getting off with one another's boyfriend.'

'I don't doubt it. No, it's not because they're homosexual. It's because, when I saw them, they were so clearly wrapped up in one another there could have been no room for anyone else, not even in the free-loving commune in which they lived. They didn't seem to take any interest in the murders, they never asked me one question, unlike the others; it's as if they thought the killings were nothing to do with them.'

'They seem to have thought it enough to do with them to do a bunk,' was Rachel's response.

'Touché.' He poured Rachel another glass of wine – her thirst after performing under the hot lights was always as strong as her appetite for food. Casey just sipped at his water.

'So, have you any idea where they might have gone?'

'No. But Moon seemed of the opinion they would be somewhere that didn't feature muddy fields and caravans.'

'That gives you plenty of scope.'

Casey nodded and addressed himself to his spaghetti, glad it wasn't he who was responsible for finding the errant pair.

They didn't linger long. They were both tired and a reasonably early night beckoned.

The following morning brought the news that Max Fallon hadn't remained in his nightclub till the early hours of Saturday morning as he had stated. One of his neighbours claimed to have passed him around nine fifteen on Friday evening, close to the alley where Oliver had been found. Had he been leaving the scene of the crime? Casey wondered. Unlucky for Fallon if so and that he had been spotted, and spotted by someone with reason to recognize him.

The demands of the case had interrupted Catt's viewing of the CCTV footage, so he was, as yet, unable to confirm the sighting from the tapes.

'I'll get straight back to it as soon as we've spoken to Fallon,' Catt promised. 'Though now his neighbour has confirmed where he saw Fallon and when and that he was driving his own car when he spotted him, it'll be quicker.'

Casey nodded, though the knowledge made him uneasy. If Fallon had left his club with the intention of waylaying and murdering Gus Oliver, it was strange that he hadn't taken the precautions of borrowing the car of one of his staff as the superintendent had suggested he might. It would have been the sensible course to follow.

Fallon was still at his kitchen table enjoying a late and leisurely breakfast when Casey and Catt arrived at his home. The kitchen, more tastefully furnished than the living room, with its granite worktops, huge American fridge and bright red Aga, spoke as loudly of money as the rest of their home.

Carole Brown propped herself against the double sink after she had let them in, careful, this time, to keep her black eye turned away from them.

'Glad we managed to catch you, Mr Fallon,' Casey told him. Fallon looked faintly alarmed at this. It was almost as if a guilty conscience had assumed Casey was alluding to Oliver's murder when it came to 'catching' him. Now, why should that be?

Fallon folded his newspaper and asked with a studied casualness, 'What can I do for you gentlemen?' It was clear from his voice that doing anything for them was the last thing he wanted to do.

'Perhaps you can clear something up for us,' Casey began. 'You told us you were in your nightclub till the early hours last Saturday morning. Yet now we learn that you were seen much earlier in your car close to the scene where Mr Oliver's body was found. Perhaps you can explain this discrepancy?'

Max Fallon chewed on a piece of toast while he considered his answer. Then he said, 'Whoever told you that must be mistaken. Mine isn't the only silver Porsche about, you know. You already, I take it, questioned my staff and they confirmed what I told you. I don't know what else I can say.'

'We are investigating a particularly vicious murder, sir,' Casey reminded him. Fallon simply continued to munch on his toast. 'What clothes were you wearing that night?'

'My usual rig. A monkey suit. I like to look the part as my club attracts high-end punters.' The latter caused Casey to smother a smile. Self-absorbed as he was, Fallon had failed to catch it. 'They expect the owner to take some trouble.'

Someone had certainly taken trouble in killing Gus Oliver, Casey thought. Was Fallon the type, he wondered, to commit such a vicious crime? Or maybe, as Catt had suggested, whatever he had done in the past, these days he would be more likely to pay one of his violent criminal associates to dispose of his rival for him. Fallon struck him as the type who had learned to keep his nose clean when possible; not for him the night in the cells on suspicion. And he would be sure to have an expensive brief to get him out of such insalubrious surroundings if ever he were careless enough to find himself cautioned and locked up.

Carole Brown had been silent during this exchange. Now she spoke up, turning towards them so the black eye was in evidence. And in spite of the remains of the black eye arguing the contrary, she told them defiantly, 'My Max isn't a violent man, Chief Inspector. He wouldn't kill anyone. Surely, you must have someone else, someone of a violent tendency, to get your claws into?'

'I'm not "getting my claws", as you put it, into anyone, Ms Brown. I just want to know why Mr Fallon lied.'

'What do you expect him to do when you come round to our home virtually accusing him of murder?'

'I expect him to tell the truth like any other law-abiding citizen. Besides, I don't think any accusations of murder have been levelled at Mr Fallon,' Casey pointed out.

'Not yet, no. But you police have a down on him because he has money and a nice life, not to mention his own string of nightclubs. It's just jealousy.'

While Casey wouldn't mind being wealthy – who wouldn't? – owning a string of nightclubs had never featured as an ambition. It was clear that neither Fallon nor Carole Brown were about to break down and sob out a confession. So unless they found another witness who saw Fallon with the victim, or the CCTV footage confirmed the neighbour's story, they were stumped for the present.

'What now?' Catt asked as they left Fallon and his girl-friend and climbed back in to the car.

'You can get back to studying the camera footage.'

Catt, who far preferred to be out and about, gave a disgruntled nod.

Casey ignored this and added, 'As for me, I'm going to organize another house-to-house. There's sure to have been some neighbours we missed first time around, such as teenagers, for instance, hanging around near that alley on Friday evening who saw Max Fallon. His car wasn't bought for invisibility.' The silver Porsche had been parked in the drive, Carole Brown's more humble hatchback beside it looking like the poor relation. 'By the way,' Casey added, 'you know I visited the commune again last night?'

'Yes.' Clearly still disgruntled at again being lumbered with studying the tapes, Catt added, 'I hope you didn't bring any fleas back with you.'

'Moon would probably have demanded them back if I had,' Casey responded lightly, determined not to let Catt rub him up the wrong way. 'She seems to have become very keen on personal possessions all of a sudden. Anyway, it seems two of its members have left their love-in. Randy Matthews and his lover Scott Johnson.'

'First I've heard of it,' Catt muttered in aggrieved tones.

'Your Lincolnshire contact will probably confirm it for you. They only left yesterday morning. The police hadn't been round to check on their possible whereabouts by the time I left. They mightn't have gone far. Hopefully, the official investigators will turn them up shortly.'

'Any idea why they left?'

'Not really. Though young Randy struck me as the nervy type. Moon told me he tried to persuade Scott Johnson to leave with him before, but Scott convinced him they should stay. Randy must have worked on him as the tempers got more frazzled.'

Casey turned on the ignition and drove off the apartments' frontage and on to the road. 'Let's get back to the station. Checking out the CCTV footage is the priority for now. I need someone I can rely on to check it out.' Casey smiled to himself as, beside him, Catt sat up straighter. 'If it corroborates the neighbour's story Fallon will have some questions to answer.'

'I suggested to my contact that the Lincolnshire cops do DNA tests on the hippie lot,' Catt told him. 'But they'd already put it in motion.'

'Good,' said Casey. 'Though as the results will take some time to come through we mustn't rely too much on them. We know there are several possible scenarios over the two commune murders: that DaisyMay was having an affair with Callender and Dylan found out about it; that Kali found

out about it – and while it might seem that there was little
love lost between Kali and her husband, she didn't strike
me as the type to take any infidelity lying down. She'd
strike back, probably by trying some infidelity of her own,
but it's possible she thought murder good enough for him.
Lastly – and this applies to any member of the commune
– that one of them took great exception to Kris Callender
cheating them and decided he had to go – permanently.'

'Still leaves the field wide open,' Catt remarked.

'Mmm,' was all Casey said. The worst of it was, Casey
thought as they arrived at the station and he parked up, that
the latter equation still left Moon and Star in the frame
along with the rest of them.

Once back in Casey's office and before Catt went off to
finish his study of the camera tapes, they discussed their
official investigation.

'Interesting that Max Fallon lied to us,' Catt remarked.
'There would have been enough people about to take note
of his fancy car. It was stupid of him.'

'True. And he doesn't strike me as a stupid man. Over-
confident, perhaps.'

'Probably liked to think he'd got one over on the idiot
plods,' said Catt.

'True again. Let's hope the knowledge that we know
about his little drive shakes some of his confidence. Anyway, he's still a definite possible. Let's consider the rest:
Carole Brown; Sarah and Carl Garrett; Roger and Amanda
Meredith; and Mrs Oliver. Somehow, I can't see this as a
woman's crime, even if one or all of them had discovered
he was cheating on them with other women. Besides, two
of them are small and slim and surely easily disarmed.
Which leaves us with Fallon and the other two men, neither
of whose alibis are strong. We'll need to dig a little deeper
and see if we can't unearth some motive; maybe the same
motive as applies to Fallon—'

'That he passed on a dose of clap to their partners.' Catt
swigged his machine tea. 'Though I can't see that forming
a motive for murder, especially as it's easy enough to cure.'

'An embarrassing condition, though,' Casey pointed out.

'Being seen going into the clap clinic, you mean?'

Casey nodded. 'Particularly for a successful man like Fallon.'

'Surely he would get the cure from a private quack? He's not likely to mingle with the diseased proles at an NHS place. Want me to check out if he's a private patient with one of the local doctors?'

'Do that after you've finished with the tapes.' Casey glanced at his in-tray; more statements awaited his attention. 'While you're doing that, I'll make a start on this lot.'

Catt was soon back, clearly having disregarded Casey's instructions on the order of his priorities. 'Yep,' he said. 'Fallon had a private quack and he's discretion itself. Insisted I made an appointment to see him.'

'Have you done so?'

Catt nodded. 'It's for two days' hence.'

'Check out Carole Brown too. I want medical confirmation that they were both infected, rather than just their word for it, which they could retract at any time. If Fallon's doctor doesn't confide in us, we might have more luck with Ms Brown's doctor – I don't suppose she attended the private practice?'

'I've beaten you to it. I've already asked and you suppose right. Seems Fallon wasn't only tight-fisted about the car she drove. She's with an NHS practice in the town. I checked.'

'And what did you find out?'

'I was lucky. Her doctor's young and hasn't yet learned how to erect a wall against unwanted questions. And although she didn't actually confirm that Ms Brown had caught a dose of the clap, her manner more than gave the game away. So it seems likely she did infect Max Fallon as she claimed.'

'Interesting that she should have been so quick to admit it. Makes you wonder why she did so.'

'If she knew about Oliver's death, could be she wanted to place Fallon under suspicion in payment for the black eye.'

'Maybe. Strange, though, if he's the guilty party that he

should also be so ready to admit to having caught the disease.'

Catt shrugged and made for the door. 'I'll get back to studying those tapes.'

Half an hour later, Catt interrupted Casey's unproductive study of the latest reports from the house-to-house teams by bursting into the office. 'Guess what? We've only had a result on the CCTV footage. Who do you think I spotted in his fancy silver Porsche not a million miles from where Gus Oliver was found?'

'Fallon.' Casey smiled. Got him, he thought. But even as he had the thought, the fact that Fallon had taken his own car niggled him. Surely the man wouldn't be so stupid? The dimmest criminal knew he would be caught on camera several times when driving around the town. Why make himself so conspicuous? Perhaps the man was simply playing with him . . .

But if Casey had doubts about these latest findings it seemed Catt had none. 'I reckon the man's too cocky for his own good. Let him argue with this evidence. This time it won't just be a case of his word and that of his staff against his neighbour. Do you want me to have him brought in for questioning?'

'I certainly do. As you said, ThomCatt, let him lie his way out of this evidence.' Catt's reaction to this latest news made Casey question his own response. At the very least, it would rattle the man.

Max Fallon didn't even try to pretend he hadn't lied. He merely shrugged faintly and said, 'OK. I admit it. I popped out for some air. The club was packed and I had a headache, so I drove around the town for a bit to see if I could clear it. That's all. The lie was worth a try to get myself off your suspect list. But I didn't kill Oliver and your CCTV footage can't prove I did. If a man can't drive around his hometown without having accusations hurled at him—'

'I don't think I accused you of anything, Mr Fallon,' Casey said. 'But the evidence puts you in the right vicinity at the right time.' And he had had the means and the motive to go with the opportunity.

'A mere coincidence. And why am I supposed to have murdered him? Tell me that. Because he gave my girlfriend the clap?' Fallon laughed. 'Carole's history anyway and so I told her before I left the apartment. She can pass her disgusting diseases on to some other poor guy. This one's taken the cure and will soon be back on the market.'

Casey stared at him. Fallon was taking this interview a little too easily for his liking. Was the man *really* so relaxed about such a social taboo as gonorrhoea? Casey didn't think it likely. What man – least of all the sure of himself, nightclub-owning Fallon – would take such an infection so in his stride? He'd smashed Carole Brown in the face for giving him the disease. What was he likely to do to the man who had him for a fool twice over: firstly in sleeping with his girlfriend and secondly being the cause of such an infection?

Aware the interview wasn't progressing smoothly, Casey glanced at Catt, who formed his back-up and nodded.

'We've questioned the witness who saw you in the vicinity of Oliver's house,' he told Fallon. 'This witness says he was behind you all the way from the nightclub to just yards from Oliver's home.' Catt didn't add that the neighbour had turned off then and didn't see if Fallon had parked up by Oliver's house.

'What do you want me to say?' Fallon demanded. 'That I waited for Oliver to come out of his house and then knifed him? Hell, I don't even know where he lived. Why would I? And how would I find out his address?'

'Carole Brown springs to mind. I presume she'd taken the trouble to get his address before she went to bed with him. Is that why you smacked her about?' Catt probed. 'So she would tell you Oliver's address?'

'No. She got the black eye for the reason you already know about. Besides, she didn't know Oliver's address. The creep had apparently been too cagey to give it to her.'

'So you *did* ask her for it?'

Fallon scowled at his faux pas but said nothing.

'OK. So you found it out some other way. I'm sure it's not beyond you to have him traced. I recall you claiming you would have killed him if you'd caught up with him. Strange if you're *not* guilty of his murder when you managed to find your way to within yards of his door.'

'Coincidence, Sergeant, as I said. Sheer coincidence.' Fallon stood up. 'I think my brief would tell you you'll have to do better than throw insinuations at me to keep me here.' He shot his cuffs. There was a glint of gold as he made for the door. 'That being the case, I'm out of here.'

Catt looked at Casey, the question – Shall I stop him? – in his gaze.

Casey shook his head. And as the door closed on Fallon, he said, 'We can't hold him, ThomCatt. You know that. As the man said, his brief would soon have him released. No –' Casey sat back – 'I think we should try a more subtle means to get at the truth. Didn't he say Carole Brown was now his *ex*-girlfriend?'

'That's right.' Catt grinned. 'A woman scorned. She must surely be keen to get back at him.'

'That's what I thought.' Casey glanced at his watch. 'I wonder if she's busy packing her stuff up. We'd best get around there before she leaves.'

Carole Brown was in a vengeful mood. She carried on throwing her clothes into a couple of suitcases while she spilled what beans she knew.

'You know,' she said, 'you should get the Fraud Squad to check out the finances of Max's nightclubs. They're far from kosher. His accountant has some scam set up to hide the bulk of the profits from the taxman. I often heard Max boast about it to show off how clever he'd been.'

Casey, having enough to contend with in the two murder investigations, wasn't interested in whatever crooked scams Fallon and his accountant had going. 'I wanted to ask you about the late Gus Oliver, Ms Brown.'

'What about him?' More clothes were hurled into the cases and she added, half to herself, 'Maybe I should slash his expensive suits. That would hit him where it hurts.'

'I think you already did that,' Catt told her. 'You infected him with gonorrhoea, remember?'

'So I did.' She shrugged. 'I don't suppose it's the first time he got a dose. Occupational hazard I would think, in his line of work.'

'I asked you about Gus Oliver,' Casey prompted.

'Another shit. The world's full of them.'

'Did Fallon ever let slip if he had anything to do with Oliver's death?'

'No. But then he wouldn't. Would he be likely to tell me when he must have already been planning to dump me?'

'Put like that, it seems unlikely.'

'Believe me, if I knew anything about it, I'd tell you in a shot.'

Casey nodded. It seemed she could tell them nothing more, so they left her to her packing, but not before Casey added the rider, 'You won't forget to let us know where you're going to be staying, will you, Ms Brown? We don't want to have to come looking for you should we need to question you again.'

She gazed sullenly back at him. 'I'll be staying with a girlfriend,' she told him. 'I'm off men.' She rattled off a name and address and Catt's pen raced across the page as he noted them down.

Questioning Carole Brown about Oliver's death had been a long-shot. And, like most long-shots, it hadn't come off. Still, as Casey remarked to Catt once they reached the pavement, Max Fallon was still in the frame. He'd had the motive and the opportunity to kill Oliver. Maybe, if they could find the murder weapon, it might still retain some traces of the murderer.

'He'll have got rid of the blade, for sure,' said Catt.

'Of course. Friend Fallon might be a lot of things, but I doubt if he's foolish enough to hang on to it. I think we should redouble our efforts to find it. That and the clothes he was wearing that night. If he planned on killing Oliver, he'd have been prepared with a fresh set of clothes and would have dumped the suit, shirt, tie – even his shoes and socks along with the knife as they would have been heavily blood stained.'

'Maybe some tramp got lucky and is walking around dressed to kill,' Catt put in.

Once in the car, Catt picked up the mike. 'I'll get the lads to check out the local hobos.'

'Get them to check the local shops that deal in expensive second-hand clothing, too. If a tramp found a suit of fancy clothes it's more likely he'd sell them to buy the next bottle or three.'

'Good thinking.' Catt relayed the message and sat back. 'Now what?'

'Now we wait.'

Fifteen

Randy Matthews and Scott 'Mackenzie' Johnson still hadn't been traced two days later in spite of the combined efforts of the Lincolnshire force. Casey, as he arrived home from the station, convinced the commune members must have some idea where the pair had gone even if they had failed to confide the fact of their going until questioned, decided he'd have to drive to the Fens once more and delve a bit more deeply. It was a depressing prospect; not only were their memories drug-impaired, but they were just as likely to come up with something – anything – in order to get rid of him; they seemed now to be as tired of his questions as they were of those of the official investigators. But then, answering questions from the police had never been their favourite pastime; most of them had been busted for drug possession too often in the past to welcome such attentions. But questioned again they must be; may be one of them had remembered something relevant to the investigation.

He kissed Rachel goodbye, told her he'd see her later, and went out.

It was with a mixture of hope and the expectation of disappointment that Casey again drove to the Fens. By now the commune members had abandoned their brief flurry into being security conscious and the big gate to the smallholding was wide open. Craggie, the smelly and over-affectionate mongrel, was out in the yard with the other two dogs: clearly they'd abandoned attempts to keep the dogs separate much as they'd abandoned their security measures, because all three came racing towards him, zigzagging between the car wrecks, as he got out of his vehicle, Thankfully, this time they recognized him as a welcome visitor and didn't set up their previous frenzied barking. The only attentions Casey received were drools over his trouser legs and the attempt by Craggie to hug him to death while breathing his halitosis fumes in his face. He escaped this unwelcome embrace and hurried into the farmhouse, shutting the door firmly behind him.

For once, the living room was deserted – even hippies had to do *some* chores if the place was to remain habitable. Casey shouted, 'Hello?' and Moon appeared from the depths of the farmhouse.

'Hi, Willow Tree. Didn't expect you.'

Casey, having thought it might be advisable to come unheralded, ignored this observation and simply asked, 'Where are the others?'

'Oh, they're around somewhere,' Moon vaguely replied. 'What do you want?'

'I suppose a cup of tea's out of the question?' He hadn't stopped for a meal or a drink, but had left home five minutes after his arrival from work.

'We're not entirely uncivilized, you know. We can run to a cup of tea, though you'll have to have it black as Madonna had her baby and drank the last of the milk to build her strength up for feeding the kid.'

'Oh? What did she have?'

'A boy. Going to name him David.'

'Nice name.' Nice *normal* name, thought Casey. It seemed he hadn't been wrong about the younger generation turning conservative against the sixties rebels. He followed Moon into the kitchen. As he got nearer, the smell of curry powder and other eastern spices became stronger, mixed with the scent of burnt toast and rancid cooking fat. Strangely, he had never ventured into the dim recesses of the house as far as the kitchen, for which he was grateful, it being better to imagine the shambles of encrusted food on the cooker and the damaged and unhygienic work surfaces than to know for sure. He hoped they didn't bring the new baby in here. But then, he reminded himself, the other children of the house had been mostly born and brought up here and survived virtually unscathed. And didn't they say a few germs were good for you? But then 'they' could surely not have encountered so many germs in one place.

It was the drugs, of course, always the drugs. And although Casey thought it probable that Kris Callender had been the only one using crack cocaine, the rest of the commune had their own drugs of preference.

Dirty mugs and plates overflowed every flat surface, along with empty takeaway containers which were piled on top of one another higgledy-piggledy rather than put in the bin. None of this piled-up detritus fazed Moon; she simply picked up two of the mugs, dunked them under the tap in a cursory wash and put the kettle on. Once it had boiled and she'd made the tea, she cleared assorted junk from two of the chairs and, ever the punctilious hostess, she took the chair with the broken back after telling Casey to sit down.

Casey, who should have known better than to eat or drink from any of the dishes in this house, forced the tea down once it was poured.

'As I recall,' he began, 'Foxy Redfern said the idea of growing the plants in the loft had been Kris Callender's. And the rest of you simply went along with it?'

'It was a mutual idea. We'd been batting around ideas of how to make some bread, seeing as how the government sees fit to give us pittances. We're not as work shy as you seem to think – it took plenty of labour to lug all the equipment up those rickety stairs to the loft. Kris only found a contact willing to put up the money for the equipment.'

'Who was the contact? His usual drug dealer, Tony Magann?'

'No. It was someone else. Some Vietnamese, I think. He wasn't very forthcoming about his identity.'

'I'm not surprised. Honestly, Moon, have you and the rest no sense? Some, if not most of these Vietnamese who are part of drugs gangs are extremely dangerous and you've already said that Kris Callender had been cheating you on your other produce. Didn't it occur to any of you that he might try the same tactics with this oriental?'

Moon just gave a shrug to this, then added, 'Hardly

matters now, seeing as the cops have confiscated the lot. And with them still sniffing around it's unlikely we'll see the Viets for dust, seeing as they're probably all illegals.'

Moon seemed remarkably unconcerned and Casey shook his head. It didn't seem possible to get through to her that they might all be in danger. Still, he comforted himself, the Lincolnshire force was aware of the situation and must have put feelers out. Perhaps they'd caught the Vietnamese already. He questioned Moon some more and learned that they hadn't confided this knowledge to the Lincolnshire police.

'Why not?' he demanded.

'I don't know. One or two of the others suggested if we kept quiet we might be able to do another deal with the Viet when he came calling as he seems sure to once all the hullabaloo has died down.'

'You're to tell them now,' he insisted. 'Do you hear me, Moon?'

'Yeah, yeah. I hear you.'

But would she obey? was the question. He could but hope while thinking that yet another suspect had entered the ring. Was it possible that Callender had attempted to cheat this Vietnamese as he had cheated his fellow commune members? Maybe so, with the confidence-giving properties of crack cocaine behind him. And if he had and he was caught, Kris's contact would want to teach him a lesson and Vietnamese drug gangs were ruthless and unlikely to consider killing a lesson too far. But that still didn't explain the murder of DaisyMay.

Casey sighed and asked the question he knew he should have asked before. 'So how long had this arrangement been going on and how did he meet up with his contact?'

'Kris obtained the equipment to set up in the loft around four months ago as far as I recall. As for how he met up with his contact –' Moon gave another careless shrug – 'I've no idea. Kris tended to be secretive and wasn't too into sharing.' Dryly, she added, 'As we found out to our cost.'

Casey nodded and changed tack to ask, 'You've still got the mobile?'

'Stop worrying, Willow Tree. I've still got it. It's in a safe place.'

The loud cry of a newborn disturbed the rare peace and Moon got to her feet. 'Duty calls. Madonna has no idea about tending a baby and Lilith, her mum, tends to leave the girl to get on with it on the basis that she'll learn through doing.' She glanced out of the window. 'There's Jethro. I sent him to the shop for some more milk.'

'Madonna's breast feeding?' It was probably de rigueur at the commune.

'Trying to. Not very successfully. Will you have another cup of tea now that the milk's arrived?'

Hastily, Casey excused himself – there had been some foreign body in the first cup so he was unwilling to risk a second. 'I'd like a word with Dylan Harper before I go, Moon.' He felt he'd given the widower more than enough considerate leeway. 'Can you go and get him?'

Moon nodded and went out.

Dylan Harper, when he finally appeared, along with Jethro and the milk, looked dreadful. His olive skin was sallow and sunk in and his hair was in an uncombed tangle of black curls. He slouched into the kitchen and sank on to Moon's vacated chair.

'You wanted to speak to me,' he bluntly observed.

'Yes, Mr Harper. As I presume you know, I've questioned the others several times.' With little result for his trouble. 'I thought it was time I spoke to you.'

Dylan shrugged – this bodily gesture seemed to have reached epidemic proportions in the commune. Casey found it increasingly irritating. 'I can tell you nothing, man. You should question the others again, though. It would, I think, serve you better than questioning me.'

Casey chose not to take his advice. Instead, he changed the subject and to Dylan's surprise, commented pleasantly, 'You seem very relaxed about the mumps outbreak, Mr Harper. Moon told me you were unfazed in the face of the other men's anxiety.'

Dylan Harper laughed. There was an edge of relief in his voice. 'Is that all you wanted to ask me? I had mumps as a boy so it didn't trouble me. There's no worries about my fertility. I've already proved it, even though I've no baby to show for it.' He scowled. 'Maybe the others aren't quite so sure of their virility?'

'Have you any idea as to who might have killed DaisyMay?'

'Could be any of them, though I doubt Star could find the energy.' His lips pulled back in a twisted grin. 'Moon, though, now I could see her doing the deed, especially if she discovered Star had found his lost libido with my Daisy.'

Casey stared at him, unwilling to rise to the bait. 'What about the others?'

He shrugged again. 'As I said, it could be any of them. It's about time you found out.'

'I agree, Mr Harper. That's just what I intend to do.'

A shadow passed across Harper's face and he said abruptly, 'Is that it?'

'Yes. For now. Warn the others not to attempt a flit like Scott and Randy, won't you?'

Dylan didn't answer, but simply got up and left.

Casey found Moon and said goodbye. Star was nowhere to be seen; he was probably asleep somewhere where he couldn't be rousted out to help with the chores.

He told Moon to give his love to Star, reminded her, with some force, that she must tell their local police about the Vietnamese drug dealer, and headed back to King's Langley.

The weather was once again atrocious. Rain flung itself down in torrents soon after he hit the A17, keeping the wipers doing double time from the spray thrown up by the lorries. He was glad to reach King's Langley and the station as his neck and shoulders ached with the tension of concentration.

He was surprised to find Catt waiting for him. 'Thought you'd gone home,' he murmured as he took off his damp jacket.

'Decided I'd hang around and see if you came back to the station. Get anything more from the great unwashed?' he asked.

'You might remember that two of the great unwashed are my parents, ThomCatt.'

'Yeah. Right. Sorry.'

'And to answer your question, all I found out was that Kris Callender's contact who supplied the hydroponic equipment for the cannabis in the loft was a Vietnamese – no name or other details, of course.'

'Bugger. That widens the scope of the investigation. Wonder why they didn't confide that little titbit to the Lincolnshire cops.'

'Probably didn't want to end up like Callender.'

'Still, it might provide your friends and parents with a get-out clause. Ruthless lot, Orientals. They'd kill Callender without a qualm if it suited them.'

'Doesn't explain DaisyMay's death. I can't see it as likely that she was meeting with foreign gangsters. She rarely left the smallholding according to the others, and if the contact visited the farm someone else would probably have mentioned it to me by now, even if only to get me off their backs. Still, it's another lead. There can't be that many Orientals living in the Fens.'

'I wouldn't bet on it, said Catt. 'I've just been reading the cops' comic –' this was what Catt called the *Police Review*, the official organ of the police force – 'and there's more about than you'd think. And a number of them have set up these drug places. It's big business. Vietnamese criminals are responsible for any number of illicit cannabis factories.'

Casey nodded. He had read the same report. Operation Atone, a national initiative which targeted the money men behind the rise in drug crime, had already found many cannabis factories, including one that was run on such a massive scale that the criminals responsible must rake in a million pounds a year.

'According to what I read,' Catt went on, 'they can get up to four crops a year if they use the most efficient growing technique. Sounds a nice little earner and then some. Certainly worth killing for. Especially if the Vietnamese found out that Callender was cheating on them.'

'Don't depress me,' Casey said. 'Getting a lead into this particular Vietnamese drug gang seems a challenge too far.'

'Got to be done though,' remarked the irrepressible Catt. 'Want me to pass the info about the Vietnamese on to the Boston force?'

Casey was unsure; he felt he would be breaking Moon's confidence. And what if he gave Catt the OK and Moon and Star bore any reprisals? But, in the end, he decided he had no choice as he couldn't rely on Moon or one of the others giving their Lincolnshire opposite numbers the information, so he gave Catt permission. Better the Lincolnshire force knew that Vietnamese criminals were responsible for financing the factory than let Moon, Star and the rest take all of the blame. Besides, hopefully the commune murders would be solved without involving any Oriental gentlemen long before the Lincolnshire force could succeed in infiltrating an undercover cop into the Vietnamese community.

The next day, they had a breakthrough in the official investigation. It seemed Caitlin Osborne, Gus Oliver's illegitimate daughter, had confessed to killing her father. Although they'd had no luck in finding her, she had come into the police station voluntarily from wherever she'd been living after she had left the Liverpool home of her adoptive parents and had bluntly told all to the duty sergeant. And when Casey and Catt went along to the interview room to question her she didn't retract her confession of guilt.

Caitlin Osborne looked much as he'd expected. Living rough wasn't the best regime to enhance one's beauty. She had a strong look of her father around the eyes and, like him, her lips were the full and sensuous type that hinted that their owner was more than ready to indulge the vices. From the look of her, she'd indulged her love of drugs to the full.

Casey leaned back on the hard chair in the windowless interview room and stared across the scarred table at Caitlin Osborne. She looked grubby and unkempt, which was to be expected if she'd been living on the streets or in some derelict building. 'OK. You said you killed your father. So what time was this?' he asked her. 'And how did you get him into that alleyway? We know his body was moved after death.'

The last question seemed to give her problems because she was silent for several seconds, then she said, as if suddenly inspired, 'I don't know exactly what time it was as I've pawned my watch. But it was getting towards dusk. I'd been waiting for him in the shadows behind a large shrub and I killed him as he came out of the house. He was startled and I was able to take him by surprise before he was able to react. No one could see me as the house is quite private and the hedges surrounding the house screen it well. The side gate was unlocked. I hid him in the garden shed for a couple of days – I needed the time to get up my nerve to move him. There was no wood or coal stored there so I didn't think his wife would go in there. I used his own wheelbarrow to move him early on Monday morning; it was just sitting there on the back path. I had the knife because I've been living on the streets in the town and I needed it to protect myself.'

'Did you see Mrs Oliver at all?'

'Before he came out and while I was waiting, I could see her in the downstairs room. She was reading.'

'I see. What did you do all over the weekend? Wait in the shed with the body?'

She nodded again, but said nothing more.

'A bit spooky, wasn't it?'

'It was dry and private. Better than the streets. And I've slept with worse.'

'How were you sure he was dead?'

'I just was, all right? He didn't move. He just lay there as unresponsive in death as he'd been in life.' She gave them a twisted smile as she said, 'I remember thinking that it was the longest time I'd spent with him in my whole life.'

'So what did you do with the knife?' Catt put in.

For a moment, she looked anxious as if scared her story was unravelling. Then she said, 'I lost it somewhere. I bought some smack after I dumped his body in the alley and the rest of the night's a blur.'

So far, it sounded plausible enough. If it wasn't for the fact that Caitlin was skin and bone. She looked half-starved and probably was. Her face was pasty with deep shadows under her eyes. Her lank hair was unwashed and uncombed. Altogether, she looked a wreck, incapable of either moving a man's dead body or formulating any kind of plan.

But then again, the outline of her murderous attack hadn't called for any great planning; merely the luck not to be seen. Though the strength required to shift Oliver looked to be lacking, which was a weak point on which Casey tackled her.

'Did you have help to move him?' Oliver hadn't been a heavy man, but he would have been a dead weight. Surely she hadn't been able to shift him along to the alley on her own?

But she insisted that was just what she had done. 'He deserved to die. I'm not sorry I killed him. I'm glad he's dead. He treated me like dirt. Ignored me all my life.'

Was this just a drug-fuelled fantasy, one enacted in Caitlin's mind over and over again until she had come to believe in its veracity? Or was she telling the truth? They had enough for now to hold her so she wouldn't disappear like the runaway commune pair. Meanwhile, they would see if Alice Oliver or any of her neighbours had noticed Caitlin hanging around the house.

After cautioning her and suggesting she avail herself of the services of the duty solicitor, Casey left the room, followed by Catt, and gestured to the uniformed officer waiting outside the door that she was to be taken to the cells.

'Think she did it?' Catt asked.

'As to that, God knows. She doesn't look as if she could lift a cat, never mind a grown man. Moving him to the alley and tipping him out of it wouldn't be easy.'

'Maybe hate gave her the required strength.'

'Maybe so. She certainly seems to have been nursing plenty of it.'

Catt, the abandoned product of a number of children's homes, remarked, 'Can't blame her for that. Her father must have been more of a bastard than she is to ignore her as he did. I'm surprised she persisted in trying to see him and gain his acknowledgement.'

'She seems the obsessive type. And then she's had treatment for paranoia according to Alice Oliver. Who's to say what action her tormented mind might order up? Perhaps living rough on the streets as she has for the past few weeks concentrated her mind. Anyway, hopefully one of the Olivers' neighbours will be able to enlighten us if she was loitering with intent.'

The Olivers' neighbours proved not to have noticed a loitering Caitlin. Neither had Alice Oliver when Casey and Catt questioned her. But if she'd been in the drawing room with the lights on she would have been able to see little outside and the double glazing would have muffled all but the loudest noise.

It was another possibility with nothing to prove it either way. Even if Caitlin Osborne *was* guilty, Casey felt it unlikely she would have to face a charge of murder. As with Moon and Star, her brief would doubtless try to persuade her to plead diminished responsibility, especially given her medical history.

What now? Casey wondered as he settled down to yet more reports. Surely they must get a breakthrough in both cases soon? In this, he was lucky – in the commune murder investigation at least. For the runaway pair of Scott Johnson and Randy Matthews had been found and were singing like caged canaries according to Catt when he sauntered in.

'So what have they said?' Casey questioned as Catt sat down.

'That Dylan and DaisyMay weren't quite the love's young dream we've been led to believe.'

'Oh?'

'No. Johnson and Matthews were in the next bedroom, they said, and often heard the pair rowing.'

'What about? Did they hear?'

'No. All they heard was voices shouting, but not the words. Still, it's a pointer that Dylan might not be as grief-stricken as we've been led to believe. Maybe he discovered that DaisyMay had been meeting Callender for afternoon drinkies and had concluded that the drinks had led to something more, as drink so often does.'

'Maybe so. Perhaps it's time I pulled him out of his bedroom again and asked him a few more questions. Probably should have pressed him harder when I spoke to him last time,' Casey acknowledged.

'Better late than never.'

Reluctantly, Casey said, 'I'll get up there this evening.' He hoped that evening's questioning brought some answers worthy of the round trip because he was heartily tired of the journey.

Dylan Harper, when, for the second time, he was winkled from his bedroom, proved even more sullen and unco-operative than the last time they'd talked.

'You do want your girlfriend's killer caught?' Casey asked. This only brought a glowering response.

'Only that's not the impression you're giving. You and Ms Smith had a number of rows before her death, I understand?'

'Who told you that?'

'That's not important. But I notice you don't deny it.'

'It was a hard time for both of us. DaisyMay had a difficult pregnancy. She threw up morning, noon and night and often couldn't sleep and that woke me up. The lack of sleep made both of us irritable, inclined to snap at the least little thing.'

'And that's all the rows were about?'

'That's all,' Dylan insisted.

'Not that DaisyMay had been out drinking with Kris Callender?'

Dylan didn't answer.

'She was seen, you understand. They looked very friendly.'

'Why wouldn't they?' Dylan snapped. 'There were friends, man. We were all friends.'

'But not anymore?'

'How can I be friends with any of them until I learn which of them killed her?'

Dylan's response was entirely natural. So why did Casey think the man wasn't telling him the entire truth?

Sixteen

If Casey found it hard to believe in Caitlin Osborne's confession of guilt over her father's murder, he found it even harder to believe in the innocence of several of the other suspects in the case. Fallon, in particular, given his tendency to violence, headed the suspect list.

But, unless something moved on the investigation, he was stumped as to how he would prove Fallon, or any of them, a murderer. And although they now had the CCTV footage as well as the neighbour's statement, Fallon had still denied he'd had anything to do with Oliver's death. It was stalemate.

He and Catt had also closely questioned each of the other suspects, again with the same result as before: lots of protestations of innocence mostly, plus the odd burst of temper. Even the polite and reserved Alice Oliver seemed to be losing her cool. Apart from Mrs Oliver, they had all followed the example set by Fallon and equipped themselves with a solicitor who would fend off any unwanted questions.

But at least things were moving in their shadow investigation. It was Catt's contact in the Lincolnshire force who provided them with the breakthrough.

The DNA results were in, as Catt revealed the next morning. 'Turns out Kris Callender was going to be a daddy twice over. He not only fathered young Madonna Redfern's child, he also fathered DaisyMay's.'

'That still begs the question of whether Dylan knew.' Casey paused. 'Wait a minute. Dylan told me he had had mumps as a child – which would explain why he took such a relaxed attitude to the disease when the boy, Billy, brought it home. But what if he lied? What if he'd caught the disease when he was a grown man and it made him infertile?'

'Then he'd have known for sure that DaisyMay had cheated on him,' Catt finished. 'Just like Max Fallon when he caught the clap.'

'Exactly. Better check out Dylan Harper's medical records. Find out if he had mumps as a boy or later.'

'I'm on to it,' Catt told him as he made for the door.

The line of inquiry into their newly-elegant tramp theory on the official murder investigation came to nothing, in spite of a smelly parade of men of the road being hauled into the station and questioned. They had the same result on finding the murder weapon. But Catt had found out that Dylan Harper had lied about one thing at least – his claim that he had had mumps as a boy. He hadn't: he had contracted the disease as an adult.

Casey had been right in his guess. But now he decided to err on the side of caution. 'I suppose it's possible he might have thought the doctors had made a mistake and he wasn't infertile at all.'

'That's one view. On the other hand, maybe he didn't doubt the doctor's diagnosis. Maybe he just went along with the idea that the baby was his for his own purposes. You said he and DaisyMay had been an item for two years.'

Casey nodded.

'He caught the disease some months before he met DaisyMay,' Catt told him. 'What do you bet he didn't tell DaisyMay that he couldn't give her babies?'

'I told you, ThomCatt – I don't bet. But even if I did, that's one bet I certainly wouldn't take you up on. Dylan must have known as soon as she told him she was pregnant that she'd been unfaithful. I think he must have planned to kill her all along. Why else would he have spoilt her in that unlikely fashion throughout her pregnancy, but to make himself look the eager soon-to-be dad? Moon told me he doted on her during the weeks of her pregnancy. That he would hardly let her do a thing. Strange behaviour from a man who must have known she'd been cheating on him.'

'Covering the tracks he intended to make. A gypsy's revenge. Crafty.'

'But not crafty enough. Did you tell your Lincolnshire policeman about our discovery?'

'You bet. Or not.' Catt rubbed his hands. 'I think we can expect an arrest very shortly. Don't you?'

Casey nodded. 'Let's just hope we have a similar result soon in our own investigation,' Casey put in before Catt became too gung-ho.

Catt's face fell. 'I'd almost forgotten about that in all the excitement,' he revealed.

'I hadn't. But I've had an idea about that.'

'Oh yes? Tell all, O wise one.'

Casey tapped his nose. 'Not yet,' he said. 'I've one or two things I've got to find out first. But when – if – I do, you'll be the first to know.'

To his chagrin, Catt had to be satisfied with that.

Catt's mobile rang just as he entered Casey's office. He whisked it out of his pocket and glanced at the display. 'It's my force contact up in Boston,' he said before he took the call.

Casey listened to one half of the conversation with growing frustration.

'Yeah,' said Catt. 'I see. Has he said anything else?' He listened some more, then asked, 'What about the rest of them?'

Casey's frustration was growing by the second. He was in a fever of impatience.

Finally, Catt said, 'I see,' once more, thanked his caller and snapped the mobile shut. 'The Lincolnshire cops have arrested Dylan Harper.'

Casey stared at him. 'And?'

'And nothing,' Catt said as he sat down. 'He's not talking. According to my source they've barely got a word out of him since they took him in.'

Casey nodded. 'I'm not surprised. He's not exactly the most chatty individual. So what have they got on him?'

'Apart from the DNA evidence that proves he's not the father of DaisyMay's baby and that he and the dead woman rowed a lot before she died? Nothing.'

'So if he keeps quiet they'll shortly have to let him go.'

'That's about the size of it.'

'What about the arguments Scott and Randy said Dylan had had with DaisyMay? He's not said anything more than that they were caused by irritability brought on by lack of sleep?'

'No. He's sticking to that .He won't admit he was aware that Daisy's baby wasn't his.'

'Damn.' Casey thought for a moment, then he asked, 'The police have all left the commune?'

Catt nodded. 'All back at the station with friend Dylan. Getting more frustrated by the second, I shouldn't wonder.'

'I know the feeling. I'll ring Moon.' Casey pulled his mobile from his pocket and pressed a number. 'Maybe Dylan let something slip before he was taken away.'

But there was no answer to his telephone call, even though he let it ring for an age, so he simply keyed in some texted questions and put the phone away. He'd just have to hope that Moon would read his texts some time soon.

'It's no good just waiting for answers on the commune murders,' he observed. 'Has anything more come in on the official investigation?'

'Not a lot. But Max Fallon's private doctor, although reluctant, eventually confirmed that Fallon had received treatment for an STD.'

Carole Brown and Fallon himself had already told them that, Casey mused, but it didn't hurt to get official confirmation.

'Gives us a confirmed motive, too. Maybe it's time we checked out if the partners of Oliver's other lovers had a similar motive.'

'Might as well. Nothing else springs to mind. Unless—'

Casey's ears pricked up. 'Unless what?'

'Unless we set a trap for Fallon and see if he falls in. This case needs some sort of a shot in the arm, so I suggest we give it one.'

'What sort of trap?'

Catt told him.

But before they could put Catt's plan in motion, they had

other tasks to get through; routine, painstaking tasks that brought no glory but which still had to be done. Reading statements, more interviews and yet more checking. The hours and the duties passed slowly. But eventually evening fell and they could put the plan into action.

'You're sure you'll be able to hear everything?'

'Of course,' Casey reassured. 'Don't worry. There'll be a couple of plain clothes officers inside the club, near Fallon's office, and Catt and I will be right outside in the car park. We'll move at the first sign of trouble.'

She still looked doubtful. 'He's already thumped me once.'

'There'll be other people about as I said; the couple in the club will be dressed to look like clubbers. All you have to do is scream if you feel any concern. Any concern at all. They'll be there immediately and we won't be far behind.'

She stared at him for several moments, then she nodded. 'All right. I'll do it. I just hope I can help you get something on that bastard. He deserves it.'

It was a sentiment Casey echoed.

By nine o'clock they were all in place. It was perhaps a bit early by clubbers' standards, but both Casey and Catt were eager for the off and could contain themselves no longer. Besides, there was always the worry that Carole Brown would change her mind if they delayed. She and her unsuspecting male friend drove to King's nightclub in the friend's car, while Casey, Catt, Shazia Khan and Jonathon Keane, the last two dressed as clubbers, followed behind in an unmarked vehicle. They dropped Shazia and Jonathon around the corner from the club. Casey gave them last minute instructions before he let them go. He watched as they sauntered off around the corner before he followed them in the car and made for the club's car park.

Jonathon and Shazia were also miked-up just in case anything should go wrong with Carole Brown's equipment.

Casey parked up and doused the headlights. He and Catt settled down to await developments. They were slow in coming.

Carole and her friend seemed to have settled themselves at the bar, to judge from the sounds of tinkling ice
against glass that carried over the mike Shazia had fixed
to Carole's bra.

'Could do with some of that myself,' Catt said. 'That
Carole can certainly drink. That's her third in half an hour
by my reckoning.'

'Just pray she doesn't get drunk and forget the reason
she's there,' Casey remarked. 'I want her pleasantly merry
only; merry enough to make a scene and barge into the
office, not create such a disturbance that she gets the pair
of them thrown out.'

They sat back and waited some more. It was another hour
before things kicked off. They heard Carole's voice loud
and clear. It had been growing steadily more shrill as the
minutes and the drinks passed.

'No more drink, Carole, there's a good girl,' Catt
murmured. 'We want the outraged ex-girlfriend, not a fish-
wife shouting her wares.'

'Shush. Let's listen,' Casey admonished.

'I won't be quiet,' Carole Brown screeched, almost as if
she had heard Casey's words. 'I'll have my say and be
damned to who's listening. Your boss is a crook, Mr
Muscles.' Casey assumed she was addressing one of the
bouncers. Or door stewards, in current parlance. 'Not only
is he a crook, he's a murderer, too, and you're all his accom-
plices. I know he got you all to lie for him about where he
was when Gus Oliver was murdered. Why would he do that
if he hadn't something to hide?'

A deep, rumbling voice said something they couldn't
catch, then Carole said, 'Where is he? Is he hiding in his
office, too scared to see me? Don't worry. I'll find him
myself. I know the way.'

It all went quiet then. The sound of the throbbing musical
beat receded and Casey guessed they must have moved to
the corridor that led to the office through the door marked
'private'.

'Let go of me, you great ape.'

'Yes. Let her go, Rupert. I'll speak to her.'

Catt sniggered. 'A bouncer called Rupert. Now I've heard everything.'

'Come into the office.' Quietly but distinctively, Max Fallon's voice came over the mike as the sound of the music faded. There was the sound of a door shutting, then Fallon's voice again. 'I'd offer you a drink, but from the look of you and the noise of your banshee voice, I'd say you've had enough.'

'What's the matter, Max? Too tight to give a girl a free drink out of all your ill-gotten gains?'

Carole's taunt must have stung, must have warned him that she could make trouble for him with the taxman if she chose, because the next sound they heard was the clink of bottle against glass.

'I won't ask you to say "when". It was never one of your strengths, Carole, was it?'

'Cheers.'

'So what do you want?' Fallon's voice sounded danger-ously smooth. 'Some kind of pay off?'

'That'd be nice. It's not as if you can't afford it with all the taxman's money you've got salted away. But it was something else I came for. I want to hear what you've got to say for yourself about Gus Oliver's death. And I'd like the truth.'

Fallon laughed. It was an ugly, threatening sound. 'What does it matter to you what happened to him? He used you, gave you – and me – the clap, and then dumped you.'

The dumping part was a new discovery for Casey.

'Why should you care what happened to him?'

'Oh, don't get me wrong, Max. I don't give a damn that he's dead or even whether or not you killed him. I'd just like to know, that's all. I hope he suffered. Did he?'

'My dear girl, how would I know? I wasn't there.'

'What – did you get one or more of your heavies to kill him for you? Found you didn't have the bottle to do the job yourself?'

There was a long, strained silence, then the sound of a glass being thumped heavily down. 'That's it, you drunken bitch. You always did have a loose tongue. You want to be careful someone doesn't cut it off for you like they did with your friend's prick.'

'Are you threatening me?' Carole suddenly sounded more sober. Her voice held more than a hint of fear.

'Threatening you? Of course not. It's just a friendly warning, that's all. You're free to ignore it, though I wouldn't advise it. Drunken ladies staggering about the streets on their own are an easy target.'

'I'm not on my own.'

'No? Brought another of your lovers for protection, have you? Where is he, then? He seems to be conspicuous by his absence. But then you never were a good picker, Carole, were you?'

'You said it. A cheat, a murderer and a wimp. My three latest conquests. I agree. It's not much of a tally.' She gave a cry. 'Let go. You're hurting me.'

'Call me a murderer again and I'll do more than twist your arm and bunch up your dress.' There was another pause. 'What's this?'

'Get your hand out of there. You've no longer got the right to let your hands roam around my underwear.'

'A mike. You came here kitted up to try to catch me out. You bitch. I've a good mind to—' Fallon broke off. 'But you'd like that, wouldn't you? You'd like to get me up on an assault charge with the evidence all down on tape.'

'I'd like to see you up on a murder charge.'

Fallon gave a slow, mocking laugh. 'Dream on. That'll never happen and you know it. Think I'd get caught – if I decided to go in for murder?'

Fallon must have buzzed the bouncer because the door opened again.

'Rupert, please escort this –' he paused – '*lady* and her little friend from the premises. Oh, and Chief Inspector, I assume you're listening to this. For your information, I didn't kill Gus Oliver. Maybe after the failure of your charade here tonight you'll believe me and play no more games.'

Casey had been expecting the noise of the club's sound system to break in, but it didn't. Instead, they heard the clip-clop of Carole's stiletto heels and the crash bang of the fire escape door before he and Catt saw Carole and her friend pushed out into the night and the doors banged shut behind them.

Catt cursed. 'Stupid bitch couldn't do subtle if her life depended on it. So much for my cunning plan.'

'You win some, you lose some. It was worth a try.'

'Not with her as the scouting party. Sorry boss.'

Carole's clip-clopping heels were advancing across the car park. Casey winked his lights and she and her companion made for the car. She opened the back door and got in, leaving her male friend standing outside like an unwanted spare part.

'Sorry, Chief,' she said. 'It went wrong. I was sure I could get him to admit his guilt. But all I got was a twisted arm and a torn dress. Maybe I should press charges?'

Casey dissuaded her. It wouldn't look good if the papers picked up the story of their failed enterprise. They would have to come up with some other means to get at the truth.

'Are you coming, Carole?' her friend asked in a petulant voice.

'No,' she told him bluntly. 'These two gentlemen are giving me a ride home. Aren't you?'

Casey glanced across at Catt and shrugged. 'Of course. If you like.'

'I do like. Besides, my feet are killing me in these shoes. I can't walk another step.' She slammed the car door in her friend's face. 'But I do like to look my best when I go to beard the enemy in his den. Don't you, boys?'

After the failed excursion of the previous night, Casey was left with few options. He'd already, that morning, given Catt the job of finding out the names of the Merediths' and Garretts' GPs. It would be interesting if the gonorrhoea that Oliver had passed on had infected them also. For the moment at least, that possibility looked like being their last hope.

But even if all the members of both married couples had

caught the disease, they still lacked any evidence that connected them with Oliver's murder.

Round and round went Casey's thoughts, but however often they circled his mind, things didn't look any more hopeful. He didn't know what avenue to try next.

He'd forgotten to ring Moon at seven the previous night as arranged. Forgotten, too, to see if she had texted back any answers to the questions he had posed. Feeling disgruntled and expecting nothing but more complaints, Casey flipped his phone open and checked his text messages. Then he smiled. Moon, that new capitalist, had come up trumps.

Casey had asked Moon if she had heard Dylan and DaisyMay arguing and she'd denied it. But when he had texted her and told her that if – when – Dylan was released from custody, if she had any evidence that pointed to his guilt over the murders, she might be in danger, she admitted she might know something.

He dialled her number, hoping she would pick up the phone. To his surprise, he was in luck.

'So tell me, Moon, what do you know?'

'It's not much. I don't know if it's even worth telling you.'

'Let me be the judge of that,' Casey replied.

'OK. I don't know anything about Dylan and Daisy arguing, as I told you. They were married or the same as, so what's new if they have spats now and then? No. It wasn't those two I overheard, but Dylan and Kris. They were in one of the outbuildings, trying to get it set up for growing more cannabis plants when I passed the door. Going at it in a furious fashion, they were. I heard Dylan accuse Kris of trying to get into Daisy's knickers and Kris said, in that sarcastic way he always had with him – "Trying? I've already been there, man. Several times." Then I heard a cry. It sounded like it was from Kris and that fists were flying in his direction.'

'What did you do?'

'Do?' Moon sounded puzzled at the strange concept. 'I didn't do anything. Why should I? If the guys want to punch

seven bells out of each other, that's up to them. I left them
to it.'

'Did they see you?'

'Dylan did. Kris had his back to me. Dylan looked wild
and mad as hell. Kris was dead two days later.'

'Why didn't you tell me this before, Moon?' How had
she remembered this when it had occurred over two months
ago? he wondered. It was another question he wouldn't
mind having answered.

'I wouldn't have told you now, but for poor DaisyMay.
And that you seem to think Dylan might do the same to me.
I suppose you'll tell the cops up here what I've just told you?'

'Of course.' What did she expect? 'It should be enough
to keep Dylan locked up out of harm's way. 'You'll have
to give them a statement.'

Over the line came the sound of a drawn-out, put upon
sigh and the words. 'I suppose so, hon. If I must.'

'Yes. You must. If Dylan was to get released owing to
lack of your evidence, you'll be the first person he targets.
Remember that.'

After he put the phone down, Casey went in search of
his sergeant. He found him in the canteen, surrounded by
a laughing throng of officers.

'Sorry to break up the happy home, but I need Catt's
services.'

The others melted away and Casey, aware the other officers would all have their ears out on stalks, took Catt's arm
and led him to his office. He told him what Moon had said
and waited for Catt's reaction.

'God, boss, didn't your mum realize what danger she's
been in?'

'Apparently not. I wouldn't have got this out of her now
but for stressing that if Dylan's killed once, twice already,
he'll have no compunction in doing so a third time if it
means he escapes being locked up.'

Catt nodded. 'I'll get on to my oppo in Boston and tell
him the latest. Should be enough to charge Dylan. Maybe,
faced with this evidence, he'll come clean.'

*   *   *

According to Catt some hours later, Dylan Harper broke down and confessed to the murders when presented with the evidence that he had known all along that DaisyMay's baby hadn't been his. Like a rabbit from a hat, Catt produced a copy of Harper's statement and handed it to Casey.

'I just lost it,' Dylan Harper had written. 'I didn't mean to kill her. It was an accident. I'd so looked forward to the baby being born even if I knew it wasn't mine. But then to discover that it was that bastard Callender's. He'd boasted to me that he'd taken Daisy out once or twice, but he said nothing to me about sleeping with her. Not till we had the bust up. I was still furious two days later. I followed him to the greenhouse and punched him hard. He went down, cracking his head on a rock. I didn't realize I'd killed him, not till later.

'I could have taken the news that the baby was someone else's, even that idle Star's, but when Daisy finally admitted that it was that womanizing bastard Callender's child, I lost it again and went for her. I didn't know what I was doing. Before I knew it, she lay dead at my feet.'

Casey didn't trouble to read the rest as a glance told him it was the usual self-justifying clichés. If Dylan had planned on killing her as soon as he had learned of her pregnancy – which seemed only too likely given his zealously attentive behaviour towards her – he was doing his best to hide the fact of premeditation. Maybe the Boston cops would winkle the truth out of him.

'The commune lot are still going to be done for concealing Callender's body, growing and supplying cannabis and stealing the lecky,' Catt told him. 'Though they're currently all doing their best to shift the blame on to Callender, seeing as the dead can't defend themselves. They're pretending they knew nothing about what was growing in their own loft. Amazing they think such a defence has legs.'

Casey gave a tired smile. 'You'd be surprised what they can delude themselves into believing.

'Now, perhaps, we can concentrate on *our* investigation,'

he said, relieved that his parents were out of the frame for the murders. Maybe, this whole case would be a lesson to them. Or maybe not. What was it they said about old dogs and new tricks? That the two were incompatible.

Seventeen

Catt's time spent in checking out the Merediths' and Garretts' GPs soon brought new evidence. And although Amanda and Roger Meredith hadn't caught the STD, both the Garretts had.

'Gives us another avenue to follow if Fallon drops off the radar as he threatens to do,' he said. 'Neither of the Garretts – or the Merediths, come to that – have an alibi worth spit. Even so, I hope it's Fallon. I'd love to see him banged to rights.' He paused. 'By the way, I was just coming to tell you, boss. The Lincs cops have charged Dylan with murder.'

Casey's ideas on their official murder investigation were ongoing. But their further inquiries into Gus Oliver's death accomplished results more quickly than he could possibly have hoped. He hadn't even had to apply for a court order, though the continuing investigation and, hopefully, the final truth, would require several of their officers to do some serious digging. He strongly suspected that Caitlin Osborne had come up with her story about killing Oliver after watching how his real murderer had gone about the crime. It seemed likely. She had admitted she had hung around the house, hiding in the shadows of hedges and shrubs in the large front garden. Who had been better placed to observe what had really happened? Finally, Casey confided his suspicions to Catt.

'You clever dog,' Catt exclaimed. 'Now you've explained, it makes perfect sense. How come I didn't come up with it?'

'Perhaps because, like Gus Oliver and Kris Callender, you expend too many of your energies in the physical.'

Catt pulled a face. 'So, have you questioned Caitlin Osborne again?'

'No. Not yet. I thought you might like to be present to hear what she has to say when confronted with what I've found out. It's my belief she must have seen the actual murder. Maybe she'll even admit it and give up the fantasy.'

'So what are we waiting for? Let's get to it.'

Caitlin Osborne had been released on police bail pending their further inquiries. She was currently living in a local hostel.

'So, do you finally believe that I killed my father?' were the first words with which she greeted their appearance. It seemed so important to her that it made Casey's voice gentle.

'I'm afraid not, Ms Osborne. We both know it's not true. So how about you listen while I say what *really* happened?'

She said nothing, so he began.

Caitlin Osborne seemed totally deflated by the time Casey had finished telling her what he believed had really happened to her father. He had no more interest in hearing the truth from her; he suspected her delusional mind would refuse to cooperate. Though it might be useful to have his suspicions confirmed, even if the words of a drugged-up and psychotic girl would hold little weight in a court of law.

'OK,' he said, once they had left Ms Osborne to her delusions. 'We'll need some spades and some bodies. Get them together, will you, Catt, while I go to see the superintendent and arrange a warrant.'

Neither exercise took long. They drove to Alice Oliver's house in two cars. She didn't seem surprised to see them arrive mob-handed.

The new turf took some time to dig up. But when it was finally removed samples of the soil beneath were taken, bagged up and sent to the lab. It should, with luck, reveal traces of Gus Oliver's blood.

Eighteen

'All your husband's women friends told us that your husband never wore condoms,' Casey directed his comment at Alice Oliver's bowed head. 'So that when he caught a sexual disease, it was only too likely that he'd pass it on to all the women in his life. Including you, his wife.' It was, as he had already figured out, their separate sleeping arrangements that had delayed him in coming to what he now believed was the right conclusion. Not forgetting the evidence of Alice Oliver's cleaning woman, Mary Clarke, which he'd finally got her to admit.

Alice Oliver sat very quiet and still. She neither confirmed nor denied Casey's claim. He hadn't expected her to. But he'd applied to the courts to get her medical files released. And he expected shortly to have the laboratory results from the soil samples they had dug up from her back garden. She must have planned her husband's death all along, ordering the new turf once she'd decided that killing him in the garden would prevent revealing blood spatters in the house. She'd probably hosed down the grass after returning from dumping him in the alley with the help of Mrs Clarke.

He voiced the last supposition to see her reaction. 'Did you have help to move him to the alleyway?'

She looked up, startled at this, but still said nothing.

Casey mused out loud. 'You said yourself you have no friends or family. No one to identify your husband's body for you or to hold your hand while you did so. And after killing him on the Friday evening, you hid the body under a tarpaulin and waited till early Monday morning to move him – the time when your loyal cleaning lady, Mrs Clarke, arrived. Did she help you? She struck me as a lady with

little love for the male of the species, including Mr Oliver.'
It seemed the only explanation. But apart from the quick
flush that told him he had struck the truth, there was no
further reaction. It was clear she had no intention of impli-
cating her obliging cleaner. Maybe, he thought, she'd
confess once she knew that her husband's poor sad daughter
had claimed the crime as her own, so he told her. 'Caitlin
Osborne must have watched you and Mrs Clarke wheel his
body out and concocted her own confession. Poor Caitlin.
Unloved and unwanted. Maybe she thought her confession
would gain her some much wanted attention, even if it was
only from the police and the press.'

Still she said nothing. Casey pressed on. 'Having your
husband pass on a sexual disease to you must have been
the last straw,' he said, not without sympathy.

She bowed her head at this. By now, she seemed to have
accepted that their digging up of her turf and the taking of
soil samples would reveal the truth about where her husband
had died because she made no attempt to lie but simply
told him in a whisper, 'You're right, Chief Inspector. It was.
It was the ultimate humiliation after all the others that
he'd made me bear. I swore it would be the last. That was
when I decided to kill him and kill him in the most
degrading manner possible. Fit punishment, I thought, for all
the humiliations he'd heaped on me over the years.' She raised
her head and met his gaze. In a firm voice, she told him, 'But
I did it alone. Quite alone. I had no help as you implied.'

Surprised but thankful that she had decided to tell them
what had really happened, Casey realized he should have
got on to the truth before now. He suspected it had been
Catt's comment about the Olivers not sleeping together that
had led him astray in his thinking. Well, that and Mary
Clarke's false testimony about the Monday morning when
Oliver's body had been found dumped in the alley. He had
lost his open mind about the case somewhere along the
way, probably owing to the many distractions the commune
murders had brought. The separateness of the Olivers'
sleeping arrangements must have infected his subconscious
and steered him away from suspecting her. But their shadow

investigation into the commune murders had eventually turned his thoughts around on the case, the evidence against Dylan Harper being the clincher. Just because one person in a relationship goes astray and sleeps with someone else doesn't mean they're not still sleeping with their regular partner. As he'd finally realized in the Olivers' case. It was later, when Mrs Oliver had been cautioned, removed to the police station and her formal statement taken and signed, that Casey and Catt allowed themselves a few moments of relaxation.

'So what put you on to the answer?' Catt asked as he sat down.

'I suppose it was the commune inquiry and the fact that Dylan had contracted a disease and tried to conceal just when he caught it,' Casey replied. 'And then Mrs Clarke struck me as too adamant in her evidence. It was clear she had had no liking for Oliver. I wondered what she was hiding. It made me think, These two cases have been entwined in my head for days, going around and around and tying me in knots for so long that it took me longer than I liked to get around to the "what if?" scenario on our official case. What if, I finally thought, someone in our official investigation had done something similar? Only instead of muddying the waters about when they had caught a particular disease, they made it seem as if they hadn't been in a position to catch the disease at all, hence the separate bedrooms. Now that Alice Oliver has made her statement Mrs Clarke has admitted that they had indeed shared a bedroom. They only moved Oliver's clothes and other belongings to one of the spare rooms once Mrs Oliver had killed him. Doubtless DNA tests on the bedding will confirm it. Anyway, once I asked myself that question, others followed: which of the women in the case would be most keen to conceal such a shameful thing – the promiscuous women who were Oliver's lovers or his reserved wife who had put up with his infidelities for years? As Mrs Oliver said, it was a humiliation too far.'

Casey propped himself on the corner of his desk and said, 'By the way, ThomCatt, I've got a little present for you.' He put his hand in his jacket pocket and pulled out a packet of Durex. 'You can never be too careful, especially with *your* lifestyle.'

'Touché, boss.' Catt twitched the packet from Casey's fingers. 'Always grateful for contributions to my love life. And, after these two cases, I might even use them.'